LITTLE GREEN MONSTER

SEBASTIAN

LITTLE GREEN MONSTER
Copyright © 2021 by Sebastian

All rights reserved. No part of this publication may be reproduced, distributed, or transmitted in any form or by any means, including photocopying, recording, or other electronic or mechanical methods, without the prior written permission of the publisher or author, except in the case of brief quotations embodied in critical reviews and certain other noncommercial uses permitted by copyright law.

Although every precaution has been taken to verify the accuracy of the information contained herein, the author and publisher assume no responsibility for any errors or omissions. No liability is assumed for damages that may result from the use of information contained within.

Library of Congress Control Number: 2021918607
ISBN-13:   Paperback: 978-1-64749-606-7

Printed in the United States of America

GoToPublish LLC
1-888-337-1724
www.gotopublish.com
info@gotopublish.com

CONTENTS

Chapter 1	Ed & Carlos	1
Chapter 2	Emmet & Frankie	15
Chapter 3	Frankie and Ed	27
Chapter 4	John	31
Chapter 5	Ed and Emmet	41
Chapter 6	Frankie and John	47
Chapter 7	Ed	57
Chapter 8	Frankie	61
Chapter 9	Emmet	67
Chapter 10	John's Lament	73
Chapter 11	The Drive	75
Chapter 12	Guadalajara	81
Chapter 13	Cellular Life	87
Chapter 14	Bus to El Paso	91
Chapter 15	El Paso	99
Chapter 16	Flight to Houston	105
Chapter 17	Houston	107
Chapter 18	John and Cory	115
Chapter 19	Looking for Philpott	125
Chapter 20	John Goes Missing	129
Chapter 21	Cory and Ed	139
Chapter 22	John Redux	143
Chapter 23	John's Story	149
Chapter 24	A New Plan is Made	155
Chapter 25	The Astrodome	163
Chapter 26	A Mystery Package Arrives	169

Chapter 27	The Best Defense	173
Chapter 28	Burning Down the House	181
Chapter 29	Game On	185
Chapter 30	El Paso Redux	201
Chapter 31	The Garden Path	209
Chapter 32	San Francisco	213
Chapter 33	Yosemite	219
Chapter 34	Ed and Cory Redux	225
Epilogue		229

CHAPTER ONE

Ed & Carlos

Emmet and Frankie had been living in Mexico for about a year when Ed decided to visit them. No one could say the longing for Emmet was completely gone, but it was buried enough to allow them to be friends. They still had art and music and a taste for travel, and the history of fifteen years together to blur the separation. Emmet's mordant wit, his barbed invective that made a conversation like crossing a minefield had captured Ed at the outset when he was a green young set designer and Emmet was the lofty playwright. *Ghost Woman* was a critical success, and Emmet let young Ed bask with him in the acclaim that poured over them. Ed wanted that night to never end, and it seemed apparent that the Warwick Hotel was the next stop from which they would not emerge for six days.

Ed knew from the beginning that setting up housekeeping was a mistake. Emmet was not ready to be domesticated. Rather he saw himself as a gourmand of the flesh, and the closest he would come to a homebody was holding court for his adoring entourage. But when you're young and hopelessly in love it's not possible to step outside and see your folly. Emmet had sped past forty-five, an age generally conceded to be middle.

Something else Emmet was not ready for. He sought younger and younger males to cling to what was left of his youth, reality continuing to be evaded. It was inevitable that Ed would be tossed aside.

Ed had a loving heart, and he went on loving Emmet and wanting him to be happy, which clearly he wasn't. Ed was willing to stick around, be a shoulder to cry on, the friend in need, and he found friendship to be as demanding as the other type of relationship and in the end even more fulfilling. Now Emmet was living with a twenty-two year old boy in Mexico, and, while he didn't allow it to be the primary reason to take the trip, he suspected that Emmet might need him. Ed's current love life was nil. Ed had plenty of sexual partners, but he lost interest quickly, and almost never saw someone a second time. At the bar they called him The Trick Machine, and it's true that he ran through the roster of available men in the Hillcrest section of San Diego faster than you could say "pass the KY". Now Ed was beginning to feel something missing. There was a hole in his psyche through which the need to love poured.

The plan was to drive with his friend, Carlos, who wanted to visit family in Guadalajara. Ed's VW was twelve years old but in relatively good shape. Carlos would share expenses, and they could explore Northern Mexico and the Baja peninsula. Ed lusted for Mexico, and it had been two years too long since he had last been. Emmet loved it too and was ready to go at the scent of a taco. Emmet and Ed had trudged through the jungles of Chiappas, ascended the pyramids in Tikal and Yaxzilan, saw the half naked *voladores* fly above the misty plains of Veracruz and bummed around the beaches of Sayulita and Yelapa. Emmet was always the Southern gentleman, always dressed in white, a cane made a handy prop and when queried as to whether Tennessee Williams was an influence he would say "I am Tennessee Williams! Now, unless you're Truman Copote, please step aside."

Those years when they lived in Hillcrest had been good for both of them. Emmet wrote a dozen plays, and became Artistic Director of the Hays Playhouse. Ed did designs for Pamela Tarsdale, the boutique queen of San Diego. Emmet placed the advertisements in the right publications. Ed got to make a television commercial for which he designed a salon and shot the actors dressed as stylists. The ads were a smash, and a grateful Tarsdale showered them with bucks and free haircuts. Time passed and Emmet was suddenly sixty. The old age he would always dread was now lurking, throwing a shadow over everything he did. It was only in the embrace of constantly younger men that he could forget for a moment what he wasn't anymore. Ed viewed with dismay the arrival of Frankie but vowed not to interfere and not to let it come between them.

Emmet was completely taken with Frankie and refused to listen to anyone. "Don't say it because I know what you're going to say, and I don't want to hear it."

"Well, it's your life," was Doretta's retort. "If you want to throw away your life on that pile of something the cat threw up it's none of my concern."

"It's none of your bananas is right. So, My Dear, please butt out." which was all very polite still they didn't speak for two weeks.

You couldn't blame him. Frankie was a dish as Emmet would say. He had a smooth, perfect body that might have paid off heavily in the porn industry, but Frankie was too lazy to work. Kept boy was the ideal profession for Frankie. He need not seek the lust of many when one could provide all he needed. Ed regarded Frankie with a wary eye and a sack of mixed feelings. He wanted Emmet to be happy, but at what price? He didn't find Frankie attractive, but he understood the kind of spell he could cast upon a vulnerable older man. Just like the spell Ed had cast in another lifetime.

Ed and Carlos crossed into Mexico at Tijuana about noon and drove amid the squalor of tumbledown houses piled thickly atop one another on crowded hillsides and through dusty streets, teeming with Mexicans and tourists. Finally they were on the open road and sped past Rosarito and La Mission and didn't slow until they hit Ensenada, where they stopped for drinks at the Fandango from which American college boys stumbled carrying pitchers of beer. Carlos lusted after a pair in shorts and tank tops, but Ed reminded him "They're straight" while holding the back of his t-shirt. Carlos believed every male on the planet was ready to jump into bed with him and only cluelessness held them back. Orientation was merely a stumbling block. So far he was not too far wrong.

Back on the road the question was where to camp for the night. Ed was bone tired, and Carlos did a lot of napping. "There's a beach at Guerrero Negro "Ed said. "We can camp there." Carlos sat up and took a joint from his pocket and fired it up.

Ed looked over and said. "I know we didn't talk about it, but I don't carry in Mexico. It's not worth it, dude. I've been stopped plenty of times, and rotting in a Mexican prison is not one of the ways I want to experience Mexico."

"You want me to throw the shit out the window?" Asked Carlos, holding up the baggie of pot. "It cost me $200 big ones. It's good weed, man."

"I don't want to be an asshole, Carlos. Just don't smoke around me and keep it really well hidden."

"Cool. I'll stick it up my ass. Then, if they want to look for it in there, everybody wins."

"I'm serious, Carlos. Promise me you won't carry on the way back."

Carlos flicked the joint out the window and reached over and groped Ed. "Anything for you, Amigo."

They set up their tent on the beach at El Rosario and made a little fire in front of it, over which they broiled fish from a one hut local market. Some clouds had drifted past the setting sun and the sky was all purple and gold, and Ed snuggling close to Carlos in front of the fire decided he liked him, really liked him. A playful breeze snatched the smoke from the fire and curled about them. The little surf lapped at the sand close to their feet. After a while they crept into their tent and snuggled under the lone, thin blanket When Carlos felt Ed's hard penis against his butt, he turned over and took it in his mouth.

Afterwards Carlos lit a cigarette and blew smoke out the opening of the tent. "You don't smoke, Amigo? You don't smoke or drink or do drugs. How do you get off?"

"Like this!" Ed grabbed Carlos' cock, but it didn't get hard. Ed was ready to go again, but Carlos turned on his side and shut off the lamp.

The morning rose from the haze, but the usually still gulf waters were choppy. Only an hour before Ed had come out of the tent and walked into the placid bay, rosy and lemon tinted water but perfectly clear. Brilliant fish weaved between his legs, and the water that he bathed over his shoulders and chest was refreshingly cool. Now the water was choppy. "Something's coming," said Carlos, getting up and joining Ed at the fire pit, where Ed was stirring last night's embers into the little fire that would heat their coffee.

"How far do you think we are from La Paz?" Ed wondered aloud.

"Maybe 200 hundred kilometers. "We'll be there today."

"We'd better get going then."

"Si, *andele"* was the Carlos reply.

They packed up and left. In La Paz they parked in front of the Hotel Bahia, a four story *edificio tipico* as a stiff wind arose out of the West. Drops of rain pelted them. They each grabbed a bag and ran for the office. By the time they entered their room it was coming down hard, and they watched the sheets of water, turning the streets into rivers rushing to the sea. They learned later it was the leading edge of Hurricane Arturo, the first of the Pacific hurricane season. They had missed the brunt of it as it veered east, north of Mazatlan, venting its wrath upon a few villages in the fertile foothills.

They awoke the following morning to hotel confinement. The rain was falling in torrents, visibility zero. The wind was ferocious, bending the palms that lined the *malecon* where a few cars crept past, their headlights refracted in the deluge. Ed and Carlos stayed in their room most of the day, going downstairs to eat in the restaurant where they could watch through the large plate glass windows the occasional straggling tourists heads bent laboring against the wind to get to their cars.

Ed tried to read but was distracted by Carlos laying naked and smoking on the other bed while watching Mexican television. *Is Carlos the one I've been waiting for?* Ed was finally admitting to himself that he was waiting for someone or something to happen. Something was missing. He was a fairly successful graphic designer, and he bounced from job to job and place to place. He was never anywhere he could call home. He had never considered being tied down. It was too much of a trade off. He chalked it up to the nature of his work, but that didn't explain his turning down several lucrative job offers. Being able to go to Mexico at a moment's notice overrode financial security. In fact it absolutely crushed it.

So, if he was indeed looking for someone, he couldn't exclude Carlos. He was way sexy enough. It seemed like everyone he knew wanted to jump him. But the sex could grow cold, routine. Carlos could get fat. What else did Carlos offer? He was fun to be around. They had plenty of laughs. He was daring and often led Ed into situations Ed was reluctant to enter, but in the end glad he did. Intellectually it was no match.

Carlos was smart. He had hustled his way to a comparative prosperity. Ed couldn't ask for Emmet intellect in every candidate for his affection, and he couldn't have Emmet, which reminded him that it was Emmet he still wanted. The question of Carlos might not be resolved on this trip.

Carlos was cracking up on the other bed glued to a Mexican sitcom on the television. Every few seconds there was a burst of canned laughter and Carlos' laugh along with them.

"How can you watch that?" Ed asked. "It's idiotic."

"Mexican comedy cannot be explained" Carlos said. "But it is geared to the minds of the Mexican peasants. This is what is inside the heads of my countrymen. Now you know why I live in the U.S.A."

"I don't know what to call you, hypocrite or racist." Ed said.

"How about realist?" Carlos replied.

They were told at the hotel desk that because of the hurricane the ferry to Mazatlan would not leave for another three days. "What are we going to do for three fucking days?" Ed asked the world.

"*No problema*, said Carlos. I'm going to drink them away, holding up the bottle of tequila bought at the hotel bar, taking a swig and returning his eyes to the TV.

"That's fine for you, but I don't drink."

"I guess that's your problem. Don't look to me to entertain you."

Ed wondered what Carlos meant. Was there to be no repeat of the other night? He was finding him more and more attractive. He was lean and athletic with smooth light brown skin and dark hair that curled both on his head and on his chest. Carlos was a little younger than Ed but not enough to make Ed an "older" man. Maybe Carlos wasn't the one, but he'd still like to spend more time with him. Maybe he could still talk him into Puerto Vallarta, but time was running out to make that decision. Their plan was to part at Tepic.

It was a bright sunny afternoon when the ferry finally appeared, and cars lined up to board it. Arturo had finally moved east and was now pelting the mainland. Accommodations were scarce and Ed and Carlos were forced to share a compartment with three young Japanese men. They showered and walked about the cabin naked or partially covered by wet towels, which was frustrating for Carlos. Neither Ed nor Carlos spoke a word of Japanese; so they weren't going to get any action from these boys. During the night the Japanese snored loudly. Ed and Carlos grabbed blankets, went on deck and huddled together under them on one deck chair. A stiff wind off the water chilled them as they clung to each other for warmth. Ed could feel the muscles on Carlos' back under layers of clothing, but he knew this was not the time to be amorous. But when? Soon they would go their separate ways. At dawn the ship pulled up to the dock at Mazatlan.

By the time all the cars were off the ferry, theirs being almost last, the heat was rising off the land. They decided to ditch Mazatlan and get right on the road. "Mazatlan is *media naranja*. It doesn't know what it is, a colonial town or a fookin resort." Carlos commented. "Too many *gringos* if you ask me. Sometime we go to Chiapas. I'll show you some things." They lunched at Rosario and continued driving South.

They pulled off the main highway onto the road that led to San Blas, a ramshackle town built in the coastal swamp. On both sides of the road egrets and herons pecked among the ferns and palmettos. The heat in the car was stifling. The air conditioning sputtered and died. Not being needed in San Diego, Ed hadn't bothered to maintain it. And while it had performed adequately on the less sultry Baja, here it seemed to have met its match. They were both sweating profusely by the time they pulled into the shaded grounds of Hotel San Blas, where they got permission to set up their tent under the trees. It was dusk and the air was thick and sticky as they hammered stakes into the ground. Suddenly, a loud whine filled the air as they were attacked by a huge and dense swarm of mosquitoes, covering both of them with multiple bites. Carlos threw up his arms "I can't do this." and ran for the hotel, Ed only a few feet behind him.

Carlos wanted to spring for a room, but Ed said it wasn't in the budget. "This is no time to pinch pennies, man. I'd rather be out in the storm in La Paz than deal with those fookin mosquitoes." Ed relented and they took an air conditioned room on the second floor. Carlos immediately stripped off all his clothes and threw himself on one of the beds.

"Our room has a nice balcony,' said Ed. "Too bad we can't go out there."

"Don't you dare open those doors," said Carlos. "Do you realize we were almost eaten alive out there? Five more minutes and we would be gone completely, not a trace left."

Cooled by the frosty temps in the room and calmed by the hum of the air conditioner, Ed thought they might get a little frisky. He put his hand on Carlos' bare ass plopped on the bed like an open invitation, but when Ed made a move to grab Carlos he was already headed for the shower. They put on white cotton pants and colorful floral rayon shirts, Carlos leaving his unbuttoned to the navel, and went downstairs to the bar. The only customer was an older man wearing a white wide brim desert fedora. He chatted with the bartender in Spanish but greeted the boys in English. His name was Oliver Reddington, and there was hardly a place in the world he hadn't been.

"Never been to Machu Picchu. Although I may yet. Not sure I can take the altitude. I'm seventy-four. Where are you boys headed?"

"Puerto Vallarta. Or at least I am," said Ed. "We part company at Tepic. Carlos is going to visit family in Guadalajara."

"What part of Guadalajara do they live?"

"The worst part." Carlos answered. They're very poor, but I miss my dear little *mamacita*. I was lucky to get out and get to *Los Estados* and even become a U.S. Citizen. No one else in my family did. I have four brothers and three sisters. Had, I should say. Jorge's been dead ten years. He was the eldest. Now I am." It was not clear whether Oliver found that interesting, but he listened attentively.

"I imagine they're all proud of you," he ventured.

"Not really. They've got their own lives. I'm just the one that's missing. I'm as dead to them as Jorge."

"And it's not because you like men?" Oliver asked. Carlos stared at him.

"Who told you I liked men?"

Oliver looked at him coyly. "It was just a wild guess. I beg your pardon for getting too personal. Tell me more about your family. How will they act when they see you?"

"Oh, they'll act happy, but I don't think they really care. *Mamacita* will. She'll hug me for a long time and cry a little. Then she'll make *Chili Rellenos de Aztlan*, my favorite.

"She's a good woman, your mother."

"The best, a saint." Carlos slipped away into thoughts of his family.

Reddington had lived in Cairo for many years. "How was that?" Ed asked.

"Sweltering. So much white. Sometimes the reflections were blinding. And it was bizarre to live among people who were praying every two minutes."

"Why did you stay?"

"Antiquities, my friend. I deal in antiquities. And what land is more ancient than Egypt?"

They went with him to his room, and he showed them a couple of things. One was a mummified cat in a small glyphed sarcophagus. It was shrunken and hairless, its mouth open as if aghast at its cruel fate. The other was a small jewel encrusted dagger.

"They say Pharaoh Xerxes was stabbed with this very dagger. Ed could tell it was Reddington's most beloved treasure by the way he handled it, and the way his eyes gleamed as he revealed its history.

The following morning they were not on the road more than ten minutes when Carlos took from his pocket Reddington's dagger. Ed was stunned, speechless. He managed to choke out the few words. "How did you get that?"

"I went to his room around four in the morning. We had adjoining balconies you know. His French doors were surprisingly unlatched. Outside no one was about. It was so quiet I could hear the little waves lapping at the breakwater. The only other sounds were insects dive bombing my ears and the hooting of distant owls. He looked like a corpse in the moonlight, laying on his back with his mouth open. There it was on his dressing table in a little velvet lined box. Who puts a murder weapon in a show box?"

"We have to take it back. Federales may be bearing down on us at this very moment."

"Wow! I never knew you were such a drama queen."

"Mexican prison is the last place you want to be. I know. I've been there."

"You in prison? Ed Goody Two Shoes. Well, slap my butt."

"It was twenty years ago. I was young and careless. It ended up costing Emmet a lot of money. Nobody's going to bail me out now, and not you either"

"You worry too much. You know what you are? You're a nervous Nora." Carlos spat out the window.

"I don't like it. It's not what I signed up for." At a turnout he pulled the car to a stop.

Carlos laughed. "You make big deal out of nothing. Besides he's not going to report it. He probably stole it. At the very least it's illegal to take antiquities out of Egypt. He probably won't miss it until he meets two more young men he'd like to seduce."

"I didn't think he was gay," said Ed. "Why did you?"

"Does a finger in my ass count?"

Ed looked at Carlos. "What are we going to do about the dagger?"

"Look, we'll be in Tepic in a few hours. You'll drop me there, and I promise to be totally clean for the drive back."

Reluctantly Ed agreed and they resumed the drive in silence. They left the coastal plane and began the climb into the range of Blue Mountains peopled by Huichol Indians and comprising most of the state of Nayarit. They had driven only ten miles when rounding a curve they were confronted by a road block. Two blue and white police vehicles were parked across the highway, and uniformed men signaled them to pull over.

"Now we're in for it" Ed muttered. "I told you this would happen." They parked and got out of the car.

One of the men walked over and said "Buenos *dias* I am Lieutenant Hernan Cortes Rodrigues. May I see your papers?" While the Lieutenant was examining their papers, his men inspected their car, pulling out seats and going through their luggage.

"What are you looking for?" Ed asked. "If we knew we could save you some time."

"*Armas*" the Lieutenant replied.

"*Armas!* We don't have *armas*. We're tourists." Just then a truck pulled up.

"*Andele pues!*" The Lieutenant sped them on their way.

When they were well out of sight of the spot where they had been stopped, Ed looked at Carlos. "I thought we were done for. How did you manage to conceal both dagger and pot?"

"Ed," said Carlos, shaking his head, "why do you always under estimate me?"

CHAPTER TWO

Emmet & Frankie

From the terrace of their apartment they could see the road below that wound between the apartments stacked on the hillside in a seemingly haphazard manner. "One good earthquake," Emmet was fond of saying "and we'll all be like so many marshmallows. Sticky, gooey mess." Frankie had spent the morning tanning his nude frame to a golden color only seen in fashion magazines. He had the smooth, impeccable skin that often disappears before twenty, but Frankie was still as delectable as when Emmet had first seen him emerging from Calvin Clement's kidney shaped pool in Palos Verdes, which Calvin liked to call the poor man's Beverly Hills.

It had been a sort of vision, this perfectly formed creature rising from the turquoise bottomed pool, shedding a crystal fountain of water, which held at its center the idealization of the young male body. That he was naked was something that Emmet was not prepared for, and he was transfixed, bolted to the spot, his mouth opening, uncontrolled by any conscious command. And Frankie, seeing him there, gave him his often used shy little boy lost smile. It was as if a steel trap had sprung and Emmet was a helpless trembling rabbit. Emmet, who to the very core of his being believed that he could charm his way out of any situation, was for the first time at a loss for words, but he was not about to let this adorable waif escape without making contact and a solid impression. While Frankie dried himself with one of Calvin's blanket size beach towels, Emmet strolled up beside him, lit two cigarettes, and with a cocktail in one hand and an ashtray in the other, offered one of the smokes to Frankie, who locked eyes with Emmet. "Thanks but I don't smoke."

"Such a good little boy."

"I'm not a little boy."

"No, you certainly are not," Emmet drawled with all the innuendo he could muster. Setting the drink and ashtray on a nearby table he reached down and helped himself to a handful of genitals. "I could play with these all night."

"Some other time. Tonight I have a date."

"Who is it?" Emmet smirked. "I'll have him killed."

"What makes you think it's a he?" Frankie protested. "I like girls." He slipped into a beach robe provided by Calvin, model host, and covered his nakedness.

"Of course you think you do," Emmet continued, determined, "but you're too young to know what you like. You're being introduced to some of the most lascivious queens in Southern California who will tear each other apart for the opportunity to ravish you. You may think you're a little stud muffin, but, trust me, before the month is over you'll realize that you are nothing but a fruity little cupcake. And, after you've been used and abused and left weeping for some cad who breaks your heart you can come crawling back to Uncle Emmet who will buy you expensive toys and make you forget all about it."

"You can think what you like, but I don't know any of these people. I don't even know Calvin. And I don't know you. I came with a friend who left. Now I'm going to call a taxi."

Emmet followed him inside and watched him take a cell phone from his jacket pocket. Emmet reached over and took the phone from his hand. "You don't need to do that. I'll be delighted to give you a ride to wherever you are going."

Calvin Clement's house was on the side of a hill that afforded a panoramic view of the tumbled together villages that filled the space between the mountains and the sea, which sparkled and shimmered in the late afternoon sun. Emmet and Frankie walked up the road until they reached Emmet's Jaguar. "Yours?" Frankie asked. Emmet nodded and opened the door for him. Although Frankie was new to the game, he knew what a Jaguar was. As it turned out Frankie's date was a figment of his imagination, and he ended up in Emmet's room at the Chateau Marmont overlooking the flesh pots of the Sunset Strip. Frankie watched from above the action on the street below and momentarily longed to be among the trend setters that frequented the street and not up here buttering the toast. Emmet reached up and drew him down on the bed and covered the delectable body with hungry kisses. They stayed at the Chateau for three days, and, when Emmet returned to San Diego, Frankie was with him.

Now they were in Puerto Vallarta, Mexico together, an odd couple in Ed's eyes, "but whatever floats your boat" he said to Emmet, who was passing through middle age with dizzying speed. A paunch had developed seemingly overnight, and nothing he did at the gym made it vanish. His hair had receded to the back of his head and now was in danger of disappearing altogether. He had suffered in rapid succession a series of elder diseases, gout, arthritis, rheumatism, cirrhosis of the liver, hypertension and had received ultimatums from a multitude of doctors. Staring into the bitter face of old age, it was no wonder that Emmet sought a last fling at youth with an adorable young playmate. As much as Ed cared for Emmet's wellbeing he could not deny him that.

"Will you come off that terrace? You're going to fry yourself to a crisp." Emmet called to Frankie, who had been on the terrace all morning, watching the road into town.

"Why doesn't he get here? He was supposed to be here days ago." Frankie came inside. He was wearing a pair of shorts he had reserved for Ed's arrival, a pair of shorts he had outgrown five years before. Only yesterday he had his hair cut by Andre El, the little Mexican hairdresser that flitted from house to house in Gringo Gulch, the aptly named neighborhood where Americans tended to cluster. Emmet was lucky to have stumbled onto a sub-lease from someone who was eager to return to the States, good for another year. Even in the dead of summer, available rentals were few. "Wait till you see it." Emmet raved to his friends.

"It's vast, darlings, and the view goes on for days. You must visit. I shall not be refused."

Emmet would have no problem wintering here. Frankie was another problem altogether.

"Stop pacing!" commanded Emmet, not looking up from his book.

Frankie stopped and turned, hands on hips. "Well, why isn't he here?"

"Have you not heard of hurricanes? They tend to blow away the best laid plans."

"I want to see his car when it appears at the top of the road. I can't see shit from in here."

"What is this fascination with Ed? You hardly know him."

"I think he's cute."

"You think everybody's cute. You thought that hunchback that brought the milk today was cute."

Frankie was indignant. "I did not."

"Then why were you flirting with him for ten minutes."

"I was just being friendly. Just because you're old doesn't mean you can't be nice. You should try it. People think you're a troll."

"Oh, why don't you just take a dagger and plunge it in my heart?" Emmet clutched his chest.

"Don't be such a drama queen." Frankie said, scornfully.

"Children can be so cruel."

Frankie came behind Emmet and hugged his head. "You know I'm just teasing."

Emmet reached around and dragged Frankie into his lap. "Promise you won't be mean to me while Ed is here. I want him to like you."

"Oh, he'll like me alright. I can promise you that." He bent over and gave Emmet a big kiss with tongue while twisting one of his nipples.

The steamroller of age was crushing Emmet now. There was no way he could continue clinging to the illusion that he and Frankie were like any other gay couple, like for instance their friends, Mark and Phillip, two forty somethings, who had been together for ten years. It was painful to finally see things as they were. Frankie was a thoughtless child and he was a hapless Daddy, a role he had spurned for years. He wanted to be a partner like he had been with Ed. It didn't matter to Ed that Emmet was older. Age never came into it. Looking back he remembered how good Ed was to him, how loving. Why couldn't he return that love? Emmet tortured himself with these thoughts. What a fool he had been. What he found with Frankie could not compare with what he had lost with Ed.

Yet here he was with Frankie, so devastatingly appealing, so cruel and manipulative. The cost of their relationship could not be measured in dollars. When Frankie came in Emmet's self-respect walked out the door. His social standing suffered. Few of his friends would speak out, but he could read it in their faces. Sometimes he even saw pity. This he could not bear.

He tried to cut himself off from those who would not accept the boy, but theater people consider themselves family and make it a point to mind your business. Finally he could no longer bear the disapprobation and took himself and Frankie off to Mexico for an indefinite stay. Few in his circle followed or visited. Those who had been most quick to criticize found other businesses to mind. Now Ed was on his way to Puerto Vallarta, and somehow he would deal with the complications that would ensue. It would be good to have Ed with him once again. He could feel his love and concern from a thousand miles away. And he knew Ed would hold his tongue. There would be no drama.

During their first year together Emmet didn't take Frankie to many parties, because Frankie's hotness caused gay men to lose all sense of decorum. They surrounded him and fondled him and tried to date him not as though Emmet were not there but as if he didn't exist. For a man with Emmet's size ego this was totally unacceptable. But to the party boy wannabe sitting around the house was a non-starter. Mexico seemed the only solution. In Mexico he could choose new friends. Perhaps lesbians were the answer.

In the midst of an argument as to when Emmet should start preparing dinner there was a knock on the door. "It's Ed!" they both said.

"I missed spotting his car at the top of the hill. It's all your fault," complained Frankie.

"Well, get the door. Do you want him to think we're shunning him?"

"I heard that," said Ed when Frankie opened the door. He brushed past Frankie and scooped Emmet into his arms. "I refuse to be shunned by you ever again." They hugged for what seemed to Frankie an intolerably long time. When they finally came apart, Ed said. "This must be Frankie." He extended his hand but Frankie ignored it. "We met at Lenny and Conrad's party. Remember?"

"I barely remember Lenny and Conrad, much less anything that happened at their parties. I was still drinking then." I'm six months sober." He held up his key chain from which six red chips and one blue dangled.

"I'm proud of you. I'll expect my amends while you're here." Emmet said.

"I guess if you don't drink you probably don't smoke pot either." said Frankie.

"Nope. I'm clean and I intend to stay that way." Ed replied.

Frankie lit a joint, took a deep drag and blew the smoke in Ed's face. "You told me Ed was fun to be around." he said to Emmet. "I'm already bored."

Ed ignored this, dropped his bag and looked around the room which Emmet had decorated with unusual restraint. "Very nice, Emmet. As I recall your taste usually runs to the garish."

"I admit I was tempted to cover that wall with an enormous sombrero, but settled for large vases and the world's most uncomfortable furniture."

They went together onto the terrace from which they could see picture postcard Vallarta. The sweeping view included the town and the sea. Emmet pointed out a high flying flock of macaws which could be heard squawking even at that distance. Well below them the heavy traffic on the *malecon* was not much more than a muffled rumble. Frankie had followed them out and announced he was making drinks. "*Refresco, por favor*" Ed said. The last hour of driving had been hot as hell, and the traffic getting into town had been horrible as usual. Now he just wanted to fling himself down somewhere, but he knew he had to put out something for his visitor hungry hosts.

Ed took Emmet by the arm and led him to the front of the terrace where they could see the street activity below them.

A man all in white was selling tacos from a cart. There was a small *tienda* on the corner from which a little girl carrying two large liter bottles of Pepsi emerged. An old man with silver hair was trudging slowly uphill, stepping off the sidewalk where it was blocked by a pile of brick and masonry. In the middle of the block was a stationery store, which a woman went inside. Some boys were kicking a soccer ball about the cobblestone street. All that was going on was enveloped by an atmosphere of serenity. Ed was eager to become one with it and shed the cares and concerns he had brought with him from the States.

They sat down at a little table shaded by a gaily blue and white striped umbrella. Ed took Emmet's hand, "So tell me. How's it working out. Are you still madly in love?"

"You don't waste any time getting to the point," Emmet said.

"You know that's why I'm here. I'm checking up on you."

"Frankly I don't know what I am anymore. Frankie's like an addiction, like a drug I can't get free of. I know he's bad for me, but I can't give him up. Besides I'm responsible for him. I brought him here. He's got me so twisted I don't know which way is up."

Ed looked at Emmet tenderly. "This is exactly what I hoped I wouldn't hear, but I knew in my heart I would. Is there anything I can do?"

"Throw him off the terrace. I'll look the other way."

In the gathering dusk Emmet's face was darkened by shadows. On the street below lamps came on, their globes held in place by wrought iron griffins. The houses on the street glowed inside their open doors. A jeep rattled over the cobblestones. Frankie came out on the deck with a kerosene lamp and set it on the table and went back inside. It cast a circle of light over the table, but beyond darkness had closed in. A few minutes later Frankie came out with a tray, carrying two cocktails and a chilled Pepsi. He joined them at the table.

"So how do you like Mexico?" Ed asked Frankie.

"It's alright I guess. I'll tell you one thing. I've never seen so many fuckable guys."

Ed noticed Emmet flinch. "I like Latin types myself" he said.

"Sex isn't everything." Emmet remarked in a slightly professorial tone.

"Really?" Frankie said. "What else is there?"

Emmet sipped his cocktail. "Music, art, friends, travel, literature. So many things. They say life is a banquet, so much to feast upon."

"Thanks but I'll just have the dick. That's my idea of a feast."

"You don't have to be crude," Emmet admonished.

"And you don't have to go all faggoty just because we have a guest."

"Is anybody hungry?" asked Ed, changing the subject. "I'm starving. I thought maybe we could go to Iguanas for some chile colorado."

"What's an Iguanas?" asked Frankie, suspicious.

"It used to be *our* place when we were together." Ed replied.

"It's gone," said Emmet. "Vallarta's changed. Big hotels near the airport filled with the most hideous Americans you've ever seen. Doretta was here last month and was staying in one of them. I drove her back there one evening, and we went into this huge dining room filled with the most gauche people you've ever laid eyes on. I turned on my heels and fled. And you wouldn't know they were there because they don't come into town. They fly into the airport and shuttle over to their hotel and never leave it and think that's Mexico, because they have dark skinned waiters in the dining room."

Frankie rolled his eyes. "Are you going to fix dinner or not? Ed's hungry."

Emmet got up and went into the kitchen. Frankie turned back to Ed, putting his hand on top of Ed's. "I'm really glad you came. I was going stir crazy waiting for you." Frankie leaned back, letting that soak in. He was wearing a tank top and shorts, and his exposed golden skin was particularly appealing in the lamplight. Everything about the way he was draped over his chair, the parted lips, the come fuck me eyes, the fingers caressing Ed's hand spoke invitation. Ed let it pass.

"It was a helluva drive," Ed said. "Emmet and I did it twice some fifteen years ago. Thank Jeebus I had Carlos along. I would have gone stir crazy as you say."

"Where's Carlos? When can I meet him?"

"In Guad in the arms of his family."

"That sucks. So many hot Mexican boys, and Emmet won't let me play with any of them."

"Maybe if you kept him happy he wouldn't care what you did in your spare time." Frankie was silent, and Ed could see that Frankie had an entirely different method of getting what he wanted.

Later they ate dinner on the terrace. From somewhere below from some radio in some house down the block Mexican *ranchero* music drifted up. A breeze sprang up bringing the tang of the ocean and blowing away the lingering afternoon heat.

"This is delicious, Emmet. Ed remarked. "You enslaved me with your cooking once before."

"Pork roast is one of my specialties. It's all in the *lomo*," Emmet said, modestly. "There's a little butcher shop on *Avenida 14 de Septiembre*. I wouldn't get it anywhere else."

"I remember in the old days we had to walk ten blocks to get meat at *Super Mercado Madre*," Ed said.

"Vallarta hadn't been *discovered* then. It was still a resort for Mexicans. Those were the days," said Emmet, wistfully. "Once a place is *discovered* it's all over. I can say unequivocally that there is no paradise in the planet that hasn't been fucked up by tourists."

"Too bad you guys can't travel back in time. You like the old days so much." Frankie remarked. "But now is just fine with me."

Ed and Emmet continued to reminisce while Frankie sat silently in the shadows until Ed stood up. "I'm really beat. I'm sleeping on the sofa, I take it."

"It's quite comfortable," said Emmet. Let me get you some sheets." While Emmet was making Ed's bed Frankie took a joint from a pack of Delicados and lit it.

"You're not concerned about the neighbors?" In Ed's mind marijuana in Mexico was still a big no no.

Frankie rolled his eyes. "Who do you think we score it from?" Frankie offered the joint to Ed who waved it away.

"I'm staying clean on this trip and from now on." Frankie shrugged and cleared the table after which he went into the bedroom and closed the door.

Emmet covered Ed with a light blanket and kissed him on the forehead. "I'm so glad you're here."

"I miss you, Emmet. I wish I thought you were happy."

"I'm okay. Really I am. I have what I want."

"I wish I believed you."

CHAPTER 3

Frankie and Ed

Ed was brought out of a hard, deep sleep by a warm hand on his bare foot, caressing his toes. Dream fragments of driving through the desert had him laboring in his slumber. In the red glow of the night light he saw Frankie sitting on the padded arm of the sofa naked save for a pair of tight white briefs. Frankie leaned over Ed so their mouths were inches apart. An erotic wave washed over Ed, covering him with tingles. "Move over," Frankie whispered. "There's room for both of us on this couch."

"Go back to your room, Frankie. I'm really tired. It was a long hard drive."

"I'll show you something else that's hard if you give me half a chance." He reached down and grabbed Ed's cock fondling it into an erection. "You can't tell me you don't want me." He pressed his body against Ed and ground his crotch into Ed's crotch. It was a moment of truth for Ed. His entire being wanted to make love to this little creep, to ravish him, to consume him. He couldn't believe that before he had not found him attractive. Now his body was on fire with his desire. It was all he could do to fight off that desire while he was fighting off

Frankie. Ed snapped out of his stupor which made resisting so difficult. He pushed Frankie away, and when Frankie pushed back, he slapped his face.

"I love Emmet which you don't or you wouldn't be in here. He is my dearest friend, and I would never hurt him. So get out of my face. Don't touch me. I mean it."

Frankie stood up and glared at Ed. "You're a shit you know. I don't think I like you." He disappeared into the shadows, and Ed heard the bedroom door click shut.

Ed awoke to the smell of coffee brewing, the same coffee Emmet made in their dreamy past. "I brought a shitload down with me. I can't bear that tasteless swill they call coffee here." Emmet said as he handed Ed a cup while he was still on the sofa. "I got it at that little bakery we used to go to around the corner from our flat in Hillside. Remember?"

"Of course I remember. I treasure the time we had together. I'm sure you know that."

"I also know that people who live in the past don't care much for the present."

"I have no complaints," said Ed, taking a sip of the coffee. "*Delicioso! Una bebida digna de Reyes.*"

"Really, Ed. I wish you'd find someone and settle down." Emmet sat down on a stool at the bar counter that divided the living room from the kitchen and poured himself a cup of coffee from the pot sitting on the warmer.

"Hey! You're the one that needs looking after. So don't go all mothery on me. It doesn't suit you."

"You don't need to worry about me," said Emmet, becoming a little defensive. "I know what I'm doing."

"Where's Frankie?" Ed asked.

"Still asleep. He never gets up before ten. The young" he sighed reflectively "have so much time to waste."

"He came in here last night."

"I know. He thought I was asleep."

"Why? Why do you put up with it?"

"Don't ask me that. Please don't."

Ed knew not to push it. He could see that Emmet was too far gone. What would happen would happen. Nothing he could say or do was going to change that. Yet he thought perhaps it would be best to move on. He didn't know how much he could take of this current arrangement.

Emmet served Ed breakfast, *huevos rancheros,* at the bar. The sitting room was furnished with Acapulco chairs and brightly patterned Mexican rugs on colorful floor tiles. The whitewashed walls were lined with cases of books save for the one that displayed a few prints by La Hoya, the Mexican Utrillo. In the corners were a couple of large Mexican urns containing bunches of tall cattails. The room was capped by a vaulted red tile ceiling. "Nice room, Emmet. You've always known how to get the best places."

"I lucked into this one. Naomi, the current lessee, had to go back to the States. I was in the right place at the right time."

When they had finished eating they took their coffee out on the terrace.

"It's my favorite time of day to sit out here before the sun is high," Emmet continued. A few minutes later Ed heard Frankie puttering in the kitchen. He came outside with his coffee but didn't sit at the table. Instead he leaned on the wall, looking over to watch the bustle below, cars bumping over the cobblestones, vendors pushing their *camarones* carts, packs of school children in blue shorts and white tops running along the sidewalk, carrying books and lunch boxes and chattering with high pitched voices. "Frankie, come sit down," said Emmet, softly.

"I don't feel like it," he replied and walked to the far edge of the terrace, laughing at something happening below."

"What's so funny?" Emmet wanted to know.

"Some kid no more than six is trying to make his burro go, and it won't. It just stands there, and the kid keeps pulling on the rope, but he's not strong enough to budge the burro."

"Why do you take such pleasure in other people's problems?"

"I guess I'm just a mean little bastard."

"Don't be rude, Frankie. We have a guest."

"Like I give a fuck."

Ed saw Emmet redden. If there was anything Emmet couldn't abide it was rudeness. And yet there he was rendered helpless in the face of Frankie's intransigence.

"Well, what would we like to do today? Perhaps a stroll through the market and then on to the beach?" asked Emmet, trying to put the pleasant face back on the day.

Ed stood up. "I need to get packed and on the road before it gets too hot. The A/C is on the fritz."

Emmet looked bleak. "Leaving so soon? You just got here."

"I know," Ed said, sadly, "but I promised Carlos I would come to Guadalajara and meet his folks." Emmet nodded, understanding that Ed was lying to spare his feelings and leaving because of Frankie. Emmet knew his friends couldn't bear to see the way that Frankie treated him. "I can't really afford much time off this job I'm doing, but I needed a break and I wanted to see you."

Emmet took Ed's hand and squeezed it. "You probably wish now you hadn't."

CHAPTER 4

John

Ed checked in at the Rosarito Hotel. A Puerto Vallarta businessman's hotel overlooking the north end of the beach, where mostly Mexican kids played, *gringos* preferring the big hotels further south. Ed planned to stay a few more days and check up on Emmet after a bit. There was no way he could stay with them. He might end up hurting Frankie. Looking out his window toward the sea, the entire Bahia de Banderas was glittering as the sun hovered over the horizon. He took the paper from his pocket upon which Emmet had written an address. It was only a few blocks away, and the meeting didn't start until seven. Plenty of time for a nap.

It was hot when he lay down. It was still early for the evening trade winds. He drifted off into a dream in which he and Emmet were struggling up a mountainside. The terrain was difficult, and Emmet had to keep sitting down to rest. As they were nearing the summit Ed saw Frankie above them holding a large boulder over his head. He awakened in a sweat, but the breeze had arrived and the sky was now dark. He looked at his travel clock which showed six forty-five.

At the meeting there were twelve people in the small room, all of them Mexicans save for one very attractive *gringo*. One of them stood, facing the others who were all sitting in folding chairs. "*Me llama Humberto. Soy un alcoholico.*"

"*Hola*, Humberto," they responded in unison.

Mostly Humberto shared in Spanish but he acknowledged Ed and the other *gringo* in English. "You are most welcome to be here with us. Share if you be needing." Ed didn't feel he was needing. He was still reluctant to be open about his alcoholism, even in a room full of alcoholics. At the break he helped himself to coffee, and the other *gringo* joined him.

"Hello, I'm John," he said, offering a handshake. As soon as Ed clasped his hand and looked into his stunning blue eyes he was smitten. Later, after the meeting they walked outside together and over to the *Malecon*. The evening breeze was refreshing after the day's humidity. White fluffy clouds raced across the moon reflected in a golden path on the dark waters. A large cruise ship with hundreds of lighted windows was heading to dock near the airport. A party boat jammed with tourists drifted past, everyone doing the *Macarena* to the tropical beat of the band on board. Happy screams of children floated past. A stray dog wandered up and licked Ed's toes. It was not as gaunt as the usual Mexican dog, and Ed thought it hadn't been on the street that long.

John offered Ed a cigarette from his pack of *Delicados*. Ed declined with a smile. "Don't smoke."

"Good for you. It's a nasty habit. I want to quit, but I can't kick two habits at the same time. Where you from?" John asked.

"San Diego," Ed replied.

"I'm from Houston. I'm here on business. I work for a construction company. I'm trying to convince the Mexicans they need our dredging equipment to build a playground at the south end of the beach. There's nothing there except one tiny house high on the cliff, and it takes a hundred steps to get up there. What a waste. Imagine the view from the thirtieth floor of a hotel there." Ed didn't want to imagine it. He knew the place and loathed the idea of a white monstrosity destroying the tranquility of the spot. "What are you doing in P.V.?" John asked.

"Nobody calls it P.V." Ed replied. "It's either Puerto Vallarta or just Vallarta. I'm telling you this; so you won't get off to a bad start with the Mexicans."

"Thanks for telling me. I've got a lot to learn about Mexico. You seem to be quite knowledgeable. Do you live here?"

"No. I'm just visiting friends."

"I think I'm going to be here awhile. The Mexicans move very slowly." John put his hand on top of Ed's. "Want to get some dinner? I'm starving."

They walked the twelve blocks to Frieda's Casa, past open houses where Mexicans were dining or watching television, across the town plaza, and, near the mercado, entered an alley at the end of which was the entrance to the restaurant. The walls were decorated with many photos and paintings of Frieda Kahlo and her famous unibrow. "The *huachinango* is very good here," Ed told him. "They do it VeraCruz style in a tomato sauce with capers."

"You'll have to translate. My Spanish is almost non-existent."

"That's red snapper. Trust me you'll love it." Ed ordered an iced tea and *ceviche*.

"That's all you're having?" John wondered aloud when he saw the tostado topped with fish salad.

"I'm too excited to eat," Ed replied. John looked up from the menu and locked eyes with Ed.

Later Ed walked back with John to his hotel, *Molina de Agua*, a handful of separate cabins on the bank of the Cuale River. In the rooms if you were very quiet you could hear the river rustling past the leafy banks. Ed was about to leave when

John took his hand and held him back. "Stay awhile." John put his hand on Ed's neck and let his fingers travel up to his cheek. "You have a nice face. One I'd like to kiss." He waited for the rejection in case he guessed wrong and then pushed his lips against Ed's until Ed responded. They kissed for a long time like that standing near the door, a breeze from the sea ruffling their hair. Ed, a bit taller than John, took over and released the passion he had been holding in until now. John pulled away and opened the door. Inside he drew Ed to the bed and pulled him down on top of himself.

The following day Ed checked out of the Rosarito and moved in with John. It had been a long while since Ed had a real affair, and he was letting go. John's body was a firm thirty years, a lean, hard torso with a small patch of hair between worked out pectorals. Ed enjoyed squeezing John's biceps and wished his bulged as much and even said so. "I'll trade my biceps for your incomparable ass any-day." was John's retort. They spent dreamy hours loving each others bodies, laying across the bed one or the other on top, exchanging deep, endless kisses. Ed was floating. He felt himself falling off a high place like a cliff or a building but not plunging, just floating, buoyed by the up lifting force of love. They paused the love making only to eat or to walk on the beach. Ed was so entranced his mind could not go beyond the moment he was in. The future did not exist, was not allowed to exist.

After the first few days John had to go back to work. Meetings with city planners had already been scheduled, and that long drive down the coast had to be postponed. Ed knew of so many places around Vallarta he wanted to show John, who had never been to any part of Mexico. The ridge of mountains behind the town harbored deep pockets of wild jungle crawling with wildlife, peccaries, sloths, armadillos, skunks, possums and an occasional jaguar. Fabulous birds could be seen on the wing or up close in their nesting grounds, macaws, pelicans, gulls, terns, herons, cormorants and even the rare squirrel cuckoo. There were waterfalls to be seen, and deep pools to swim. So much to share with this new beau but non-stop love consumed all their time. Meanwhile Ed resented every obligation that took John away from him.

During the days when John was in negotiations with the Mexicans, Ed wandered from beach to bar and back again. He walked up and down the *malecon* not even noticing the hundreds of beautiful boys in their tight, bikini briefs. Gorgeous tans and flaunted six packs were wasted on him. His head was bursting with images of John and his voice, his words. Sometimes he had non-alcoholic cocktails at Tillie's near the Oceano Hotel. Sometimes he found himself in the *mercado*, and once he bought floral print rayon shirts for himself and John. Another time bought a hat and *Delicados* for John.

John wanted to know where they could score some pot. "Not here," Ed told him. "But we can score some in Yelapa, a village about twenty miles from here."

"Should we rent a car?"

"There's no road. We have to get a boat. There's a *panga* that goes there every day at noon from the beach next to the Rosarito. We can go tomorrow if you don't have any meetings."

In the morning they were up early and had a light breakfast at Bambino's before walking across town to the Rosarito where people were already gathering on the beach below, lounging among their bags and bundles in the shadow of the sea wall that separated tranquil beach and sea from the busy *malecon*..

Two *gringas* smoked and laughed, and one made eye contact with Ed, who took John's hand. She looked away. Two leathery Mexicans, wearing pants rolled to the knees and *huaraches* turned over the boat waiting in the sand and made it ready for the water. They pushed it into the surf and one sat in the stern while the other held it steady against the rocking of the waves while the people climbed aboard and sat

35

on the benches. A small Mexican boy ran up and jumped in the bow. The other Mexican still on the sand pushed them off and waved.

The morning overcast was burning off and the gray green world turned blue green. The reflected jungle turned the water green-black, and the launch sped over the glassy surface thump bumping on the rising swells, spraying white foam behind them. Ed put his arm around John to hold him steady and relived the thrill of the ride playing upon John's smiling face. The boat hugged the shore where pelicans sat on rocks covered with white droppings. The boat made the turn into Yelapa's bay, and Ed glanced to see John's face. It was a good sized inlet between two lush mountain ridges. A river with a lagoon flowed between those mountains and into the bay. The surf lapped gently against white sand, and thatched roofed house were stacked on the hillsides. The launch passed the village, a cluster of concrete buildings with red tile roofs, and docked near the beach, where some men pulled them up onto the sand.

Ed and John walked a mile up river, passing some houses made of sticks and some small airless boxes made of concrete. Dogs announced their passing with sharp barks. Children in dirty underpants played in the mud, and at the bend of the river women crouched in the flow, beating their laundry on large flat boulders. They stopped at a little *tienda* and shared a cold soda and a soft, pink gooey cookie which John bit in half and shoved into Ed's reluctant mouth. Then they kissed in the shade of a tree. "No one cares," Ed said. "They think all the *gringos* are crazy here. But they don't like nudity. And half the *gringos* run around naked in their *casas*. There's something about the tropics that makes white people want to strip off their clothing. I used to come here with Emmet, my ex. At our place here we never wore a stitch. It was just too damn hot.... for clothes I mean. Escamillo, our *mozo*, used to spy on us when we fucked on our hanging bed. He was out there in the bushes masturbating. We could see the tip of his hat poking above the bush. He was a piece of work that Escamillo. He beat his daughter, and one wall of his hut was made up of used kotex boxes."

They stopped at the gate of a small brick house with a large porch and a tile roof. Ed pulled the cord attached to the wood gate and a bell rang softly in the house. A tall, older man came out on the deck. "Hola, Don Francisco!" The man's face brightened as he recognized Ed. "His grandfather fought in the Revolution," Ed said to John, to whom he introduced to Don Francisco as they came up the steps onto the porch, shaded by two large, spreading sycamore trees. They sat down at a round wooden table on the deck, and Don Francisco went inside the house, and returned presently with a tray and three glasses of iced tea. He was followed outside by a friendly, little dachshund coming out to greet them. "Ah, Emma! So nice to see you." Ed gave her a vigorous patting. "She's the only dog I've seen that wags her entire body." John reached down to pet her, and she promptly jumped in his lap. "She loves everybody," said Don Francisco.

They chatted a little about politics and goings on in the village. He was a trove of information about federal, state and local government and even the non-existent governing body of the village. "Ah, but what do I know?" was his usual disclaimer. "Put out to pasture like an old *caballo.*"

"You love it," said Ed. "You wouldn't be here if you didn't."

"Life is like a rushing river. When a man is young he longs to be in the midst of it, even to risk letting it carry him away. He battles the currents and learns to avoid passing debris and thinks he has shown that river a thing or two. But when he is older he is content to sit on the bank and appreciate the things around him. The happy cries of children playing. The lovers kissing in the shadows. The sudden, breeze that comes off the water after a hot, breathless day. The splendid gold and purple of a sunset sky, the chorus of frogs after a surprise shower. Thunder and lightening. Nature is a major player out here. She gets lost in the city." For a moment he seemed lost in contemplation.

After awhile Ed got to the point. "We need to score some pot. Is there any in town?"

"Claudio went into the mountains last week. Maybe he's back. You know where he lives?"

In parting they shook hands solemnly, not sure they would ever see each other again. They continued up the trail another half mile through pasture land and sometimes thick forest. Houses were further apart, and those were cruder and less appealing. Ed stopped at a gate beyond which was a large grassy field with several fat cows enjoying a midday lunch and a small thatch covered hut nestled amid a grove of trees in front of a large hill from which a thin stream of water fell about twenty feet. Claudio saw them coming and waved from his hard packed dirt yard. They passed a white horse tied to a tree. "How come you got Maria Stella all tied up like that?" Ed asked Claudio after the greeting formalities.

In cracked English Claudio, with a toothless grin explained, "She run off. Don't you ask me. Gone *muy loco*. I find her up by Chacmulo. *Mucha pulga.*

Now I no take chances."

John sat in the only chair, a straight backed wooden one, in the yard, while Claudio sat on a log with a board nailed on top of it which he used to roll a joint. Ed plopped in a hammock slung between two trees. Claudio lit the joint and handed it to John who took a deep drag and offered it to Ed who waved it away.

Claudio looked amazed. "No believe *mi ojos. No quieres mota?.*"

"I quit." Ed said. "No *bebidas,* no *cigarros,* no *mota.*"

"You may as well be *muerte, amigo.*" said Claudio.

Claudio brought John a big bag of weed, much more than he could smoke in the time he had remaining in Mexico. As they were parting, Claudio took Ed aside and asked "*Tu amigo es muy simpatico?*"

"*Si muy.*"

Claudio grinned and gave Ed an affectionate and conspiratorial punch in the shoulder. Ed wondered why Claudio took such delight in his love life. He probably lacked one of his own if you didn't count the goats, Ed concluded. John stowed the pot in his backpack and was ready to head back down the trail, but Ed said "I want to show you something" and they continued up the dirt path.

After they crossed the river a second time there were no more houses and the trail was steeper. The river could not be seen through the thick vegetation but its sonorous rush told them it was close at hand. "Here!" said Ed. A narrow trail through the leafy tangle took them to the sandy bank of the white foaming river rushing past. "Strip." said Ed. "Put your clothes on that rock," he said pointing to a large boulder. They undressed together, but John left his boxer shorts on. "Those too." said Ed.

John was reluctant. "You said they didn't like nudity."

"They don't, but I do, especially yours." John dropped his shorts tossed them with the rest of his clothes, and Ed stood looking at him for a few moments before saying "Let's go in." He took John's hand and led him into the water. The river was fairly shallow, no more than thigh deep, but the current was strong.

"Don't let it pull you along or you'll go over the fall." Ed warned. They struggled upstream a ways to a cluster of large boulders that the river was boiling over. "We call these the Jacuzzis" Ed shouted over the noise. Once amid the boulders Ed pressed his body against John's and let the water give them a massage. "I dreamed of being here with you," he shouted in John's ear.

A short ways downstream on a large flat rock, Ed fucked John and afterwards they lay in the sun and watched the river plunge over the lip of the fall about thirty feet away. The jungle with its dangling vines towered above them, and exotic birds flitted among its upper reaches. John lay on his stomach dozing and Ed sitting up studied the contours of his body, the sinewy shoulders, the straight back, the smooth, round, firm buttocks that Ed had taken so much pleasure in fondling, the sturdy thighs and muscular calves that contained the only hair on his body. John rolled on his back and said "I wish I had a smoke" before dozing off again. Ed dropped into the river and crossed over to the bank and walked to the place where they had left their clothes and returned with John's cigarettes and matches.

When John sat up Ed lit his cigarette. "I'm getting ridiculously fond of you." Ed said.

CHAPTER 5

Ed and Emmet

It was a Wednesday afternoon and Vallarta was not quite awake from its siesta. John was caught up in an extended negotiation with the mayor and assorted *funcionarios de la ciudad*. Business was transacted between shots of tequila and lighting of *cigarros* in the City Hall that towered over what was basically a one story city. The *oficiars de ciudad*, sensing the nearness of agreement with only minor details still needed to be worked out, had begun their celebrations. This entailed frequent backslapping, trays of taquitos, more backslapping, hand shaking, embraces and finally dancing. At first John refused to drink, but some of the men looked offended, and, when the project seemed threatened, he succumbed to their pressure. He could always go back "on the wagon" after this was all over, but he was careful not to let himself get drunk, sloppy or stupid. He could screw up the deal and, worse, could blow it with Ed. He had never met anyone even remotely like him, and he, was to put it mildly, totally infatuated.

Ed was in that stage of an affair where even a moments separation is unbearable. He wandered the hot sidewalks and cobblestone streets with all thoughts fixated on his lover. He brushed into other pedestrians and nearly smacked into a metal lamppost supporting a wrought iron griffin in the town plaza. He found shade at Tio Mateo's, an outdoor cantina, where aching tourists could cool their heels in the little koi pond and stow their numerous packages under wicker chairs. While nursing a *limonada* beneath a spreading avocado tree John's face loomed up from his thoughts, the beard shadowed dimpled chin, lush lips, full and soft, waiting to be kissed, the nose, not prominent but nicely shaped and not calling attention to itself. Only the lake blue eyes hinted at a mysterious side. John's presence projected a calmness, an almost passivity which in turn produced a protective response in a caring partner. Ed was aware of this inclination, and he was careful not to let it grow into possessiveness. John's hair was black and straight and neatly combed, and Ed could not resist mussing it at every opportunity. Inevitably, his thoughts continued to John's body and traveled down the flat hard chest to the sexual organs that had kept him in an almost constant state of arousal since he had met him. He was brought rather suddenly out of this reverie by a familiar voice.

"Why there you are, you scoundrel. I thought you were in Guad."

"I was," Ed lied. "I just got back."

Emmet sat down beside him. "I know it's Frankie. Everyone is avoiding me like a venereal disease. It appears I can't have my fun and my friends too."

"Frankly, Frankie is a bit of a hard pill to swallow," said Ed. "The truth is I've met someone."

"That's wonderful!" Emmet leaned forward and squeezed Ed's knee. "Tell Mother all about it."

"You might find him completely ordinary," Ed began, "but all I can think about is that he might finish his business here soon. Then he'll have to return to Houston."

"So? You go to Houston."

"What would I do there? Start over? My work is in San Diego, all my clients, my reputation. I was becoming successful. People wanted my designs. Word was getting around in the right circles. Let's face it. I'm no good for anywhere but here and Hillside."

Emmet shook his head, almost exasperated. "You'll move in with him.

You'll make him a wonderful cozy nest. You'll make love all night every night."

"He hasn't even hinted at anything of the sort. We've more or less avoided the subject of his leaving."

Emmet took Ed by the shoulders. "Darling, is he as crazy about you?"

"I think so. We've been inseparable for two weeks. He's extraordinary in bed."

Emmet looked at him wistfully. "As I recall you're pretty good yourself."

"Once upon a time I was in love with you too." Ed blushed. "But you brushed me off."

"Darling, you know better than anyone that the only thing that excites me is cheap trash. You were always too good for me."

"I could have been good for you, Emmet."

"You were good for me, but you know as well as I that nothing lasts." The waiter appeared with another lemonade for Ed and a martini for Emmet. "Salud!" said Emmet, raising his cocktail. They clinked glasses.

"It's a shame you've stopped writing," said Ed. "You were great once."

"I don't feel the call. You can't force it. If you do, all you get is shit."

Ed leaned forward and kissed Emmet on the forehead. "I still love you, you know."

Emmet reddened a little. He had grown unused to affection. "That's what happens when you're in love. It's like a fountain inside of you, bubbling over onto everyone you know." Abruptly he changed the subject. "Do you ever see any of the old gang? How is Doretta? What about Mae?"

"Doretta is Doretta. Proclaiming everlasting love one day; stabbing you in the back the next. Mae is just as crusty as ever. I try to stop in on her a couple of times a week. She is getting up there."

"I wish she would move here. There's a whole nest of lesbians in Gringo Gulch. She'd fit right in."

"I don't think she likes being separated from Hillside's Kaiser. She thinks the only doctors in Mexico are witch doctors. How old is she now?" Ed asked.

"Around seventy I think. She looks eighty-three. The bag has lived, my dear."

"I remember she used to take care of us in our twinky days."

Emmet took umbrage. "I was never a twink. I was born a daddy."

Just then John appeared. He walked over to their table and kissed Ed on the mouth. Then he shook hands with Emmet who said "Of course, you're John. I wondered why a movie star was kissing Ed."

"He hasn't a clue about his beauty," commented Ed. "They don't know how to appreciate gorgeous men in Houston."

"Dreadful place," said Emmet. "I was there once. It's the capitol of humidity."

John smiled shyly as he sat down. "I've had a few admirers."

"So modest," said Emmet. "It's half your charm. Don't ever change."

"So how did it go?" asked Ed.

"I don't know. With them everything is a cause for *bebidas*?"

"Do I detect the familiar aroma of tequila?" Emmet said, sniffing.

"It couldn't be helped. They can be very insistent. I would like to go to a meeting tonight if it's okay with you."

"Sure, babe. *No problema!*"

"Anyway celebration is premature. There's a whole bunch of details to work out."

"Good!" Ed replied. "I hope it goes on forever."

"And I couldn't be happier," John added.

"Well, I can see you two are head over heels," Emmet said, rising and taking his leave, "and three's a crowd. But I insist you both come to dinner at Casa Emmet. I'll invite the lesbos next door. Cas and Tilda. You'll love them. They're a hoot. I won't take no for an answer. Shall we say Tuesday?"

On the walk back to the hotel Ed put his arm around John and his mouth up to his ear which he nibbled gently before saying, "I'm sorry. I couldn't refuse. Emmet would have been so hurt."

"I don't mind. I like him. He's really sweet."

"You haven't met Frankie yet," Ed said.

CHAPTER 6

Frankie and John

On Tuesday the Emmet labeled lesbos, one with tequila the other with rum, arrived, stirring the air with chatter, as they came out of their apartment next door and rang Emmet's bell. John opened the door and Cas stuck her foot in. "Don't try to shut the door. That's what people usually do the minute they see me," she cackled. "My aren't you a cutie. They said you were a looker, but I had no *ideah*, my *deah*." She fanned herself as if she were overcome with hot flashes. Tilda was smaller, shyer, and, while not pretty, had a sensitivity that made her appealing. Cas put her arm around her and said, "I'll mind you to stay away from my honey. I suspect you're quite the charmer."

John laughed. "You don't have to worry. I like men."

"Well, I doubt you'd be here if you didn't," Cas shrieked.

John took the bottles and welcomed them inside. "Frankie's making drinks."

"Ah, the imp from hell. I'm surprised Emmet hasn't pushed him off the terrace."

"He's not so bad," John said. "He's just a kid."

"Kid my ass! Don't say I didn't warn you."

Emmet welcomed them into the fold, as they joined the others on the terrace. Ed was talking to Ethel Fettle, the older downstairs neighbor, who naturally knew the *girls*. Cas gave her a hug. "I call her a fine Fettle of Fish." She slapped Ethel's butt and cackled at her own joke. Meat was already sizzling on the portable grill, and it's aroma filled the still, humid air. Frankie, wearing tight cut-offs and a see through tank top, appeared with a tray filled with frosted glasses. "Martuna's anyone?"

Ed watched Frankie mingling with the guests, serving drinks, setting the table, all the while keeping up with the conversation and thus far not insulting anyone. Ed thought he must be on his very best behavior. At one point, while serving a drink to Ethel he caught Ed watching him. Later he whispered in Ed's ear, "Better keep an eye on your pretty boy. I'm going to pluck him before the evening's over."

"You stayed at the Rosarito?" Cas screeched. "It's so bad even the scorpions avoid it."

"Just one night. John rescued me and swept me off to the Molina." Ed replied. "It does lack a few amenities."

"Well, thank Gertrude," she chortled. "I've heard tourists check in there and are never seen again."

"Don't listen to Cas. She makes stuff up." Tilda said, rocking a bit on her second martini.

"The Molina's quite nice," Emmet ventured to say. "The grounds are lovely, and once there was the cutest little *mozo* who insisted on making my bed with him in it."

"Emmet's the horniest person I know," Cas remarked. "I think it's a disease. Probably fatal."

"I'll outlive all you bitches. Just wait." He handed his glass to Frankie for a refill.

"Don't drink too much," Ed started to say but caught himself before slipping into an old habit.

"If there's one thing my Frankie can do it's make a good martini. Isn't that right, my love?"

"Nothing's too good for my Emmet" Frankie cooed, kissing Emmet's bald pate.

"I may vomit," said Cas.

"I can't finish mine. I'm already buzzed," said Tilda, handing her glass to Cas who finished it for her.

"So, Ed," asked Ethel, "how do you know our Emmet?"

"I was his Emmet long before I knew you, my dearest Ethel. We even lived together once upon a time. They were wonderful years, but they seem like a dream now."

"Sounds like a big fairy tale to me," interjected Frankie. "Did you live in an enchanted castle and have hundreds of servants?"

"Toodle off, sonny, and let the grown-ups have their conversation," said Cas, dismissing him with a wave of her hand.

"Zip it, bitch, or I'll put oven cleaner in your next martini."

"Por favor," said Emmet, holding his head between his hands. "It hurts my head when you two fight."

"Well, she started it," said Frankie, taking exception.

"I don't care. Just stop," said Emmet, almost shouting. Frankie gave him a dark look.

Ed was keeping an eye on John, who was still "off the wagon" and having his second drink. John excused himself to go to the bathroom. When he came out Frankie was waiting by the door. "Come. I want to show you something." He led him to the bedroom which was next to the bathroom. He drew John into the closet and showed him the peephole through which you could see into the bathroom. "I drilled it myself. I was watching you pee. You've got a nice dick. I want to suck it." He began groping John who tried to wriggle free.

"I should get back." Frankie blocked his passage and simultaneously unbuttoned his shorts, quickly getting his hand inside his briefs. Despite his objections John could not help getting hard. Frankie went down on his knees and took John's penis in his mouth. John's will to resist gave way as pleasure took over.

"Yum!" muttered Frankie with his mouth full. "I'll say this for Ed; he's got good taste."

Ed walked into the room and saw them in the open closet. John jerked away and quickly buttoned his pants. Ed didn't say anything. Instead he turned to walk out of the room.

Frankie followed him out. "It's my fault" said Frankie. "I forced myself on him."

This was the moment when everything changed for Ed and John as Ed realized the impossible romanticism of his feelings. John rushed to catch up to Ed, to seek forgiveness, to somehow remain unchanged in Ed's eyes. He stumbled through his embarrassment, and Ed put his arm around him and kissed away the worry in his eyes. "I don't blame you. That little fucker is dangerous." He took John by the shoulders. "Look! If you want to play around I'm not going to stop you. That's on you, but Frankie is off limits."

"I don't want to play around. I'm nuts about you, Ed. He took me by surprise."

"Just be aware. He's dangerous. He likes to mess with people. Someone's boyfriend is a perfect target." Ed took John in his arms and said softly in his ear. "Are you my boyfriend?." John, whose head was buried in Ed's shoulder, hugged Ed tightly, his tears wetting Ed's shoulder, "Yes, if you still want me."

"Of course, I still want you. I want you more than ever." Ed replied.

When Ed and John returned to the terrace Frankie was in the kitchen fixing more drinks. Ed stepped inside and confronted him. "Stay away from him."

Frankie smirked. "You tell him to stay away from me."

Ed and John walked back to the Molina in awkward silence. Ed knew they had to get through this first act of unfaithfulness on John's part. Ed knew it would happen again. John was younger and surrounded by temptation. How could he deny John the abandon of youth? It was late and their footsteps echoed on the empty cobblestones. A drunk Mexican staggered out of a *cantina* to the accompaniment of teary *ranchero* music and fell into some weeds at a dormant construction site. "Shouldn't we check to see if he's okay?" John asked.

"If he's still there in the morning someone will pick him up and point him toward his *casa*. Usually by this time there's a trail of fallen drunk Mexicans leading up to the *cantina*. It's almost a Saturday night tradition."

"But it's only Tuesday."

"Then maybe not many but always some."

"Crazy country," commented John.

"No crazier than anywhere else," Ed said, "when you get to know it.

Mexicans are the kindest people I've ever met. If you ask one for directions they'll walk blocks out of their way to make sure you get where you're going. They're generous. If you're their guest they will lavish food upon you, even if they have little to eat themselves. And, you must eat in order not to offend them. It takes a certain skill to navigate their customs and still...." John stopped and held Ed back from continuing.

"I"m sorry," he said to Ed.

"For what?"

"For what happened with Frankie."

"Forget it. We don't need to talk about it. It just can't happen again."

When they got back to John's cottage John said he was tired and needed to sleep. "Drama always does drains me." They stood for a long while kissing in the shadows before John opened the door and slipped inside. Ed walked back across town which was now almost entirely shut down. Occasional bars emitted a momentary raucous commotion, a mixture of loud music and louder voices, but they did little to alter the gentle stillness of the tropical night. A light breeze rustled the palms in the plaza, and from the *malecon* the surf's rhythmic roar shattered the evening silence. Even the day's clamorous traffic was reduced to the rattle of an occasional automotive heap. Ed, lost in thoughts of John, failed to notice the enticing boys on the sidewalk, sitting on carved iron benches or wandering about, some smoking, some not, but all noticing Ed as he passed.

He was reviewing in his mind the events of the evening, trying to determine if there was a subtle, hardly noticeable difference in John's kisses. Was there a degree less passion? Or was he just tired and drained as he said? He hoped he could reclaim his room at the Rosarito. He would have to wake up the night manager. Ed knew that hotels in Puerto Vallarta were accustomed to expecting the unexpected. Long delayed flights arriving in the middle of the night and disgorging hosts of disgruntled passengers were not unheard of. Far from it.

This would be the first night Ed and John had not spent together since they met. He didn't like the idea of being alone with his thoughts. He hated the sudden uncertainty. He knew he wouldn't sleep. The night manager of the Rosarito, Jorge, greeted Ed like an old friend and handed him the key before he asked for it.

He was almost glad to be back in his old familiar room. He flopped on the bed without bothering to undress, but sleep wouldn't come. A stiff breeze had blown away the last fluffy cloud, and the moon beamed through his open window right into his eyes.

In the morning Ed stopped at a *panderia* and bought a bag full of pastries. By this time the city had come alive and traffic inched through the narrow streets. He cut through the *mercado* and stopped at a stall for *cafe con leche*, taking it to go, anxious to get to John, anxious to make things right again.

He knocked on the door to John's cabin before noticing the piece of paper pinned to the door. Scrawled upon it were two words "Gone Shopping." Ed tried the door but it was locked. *What now?* Should he wait? He might be back any minute. Should he look for him? Puerto Vallarta wasn't all that big. There weren't that many places he might be. The market, the beach, the little shops on the *malecon,* one of the little cafes they liked, a bar (not this early). He might even be at the Rosarito, looking for Ed. He decided to get another coffee and some breakfast and check back in an hour. He tossed the bag of pastries in a bin marked basura and went inside a small cafe.

Ed picked at his *huevos rancheros.* He didn't have much appetite. By the time he decided he was finished his tortillas were stiff and yellow egg had congealed on his plate. The young woman brought his check, and he left some bills on the table and departed the cafe. The door to John's room was open, and Ed's heart did a small leap, but, when he looked in, it was the *mozas,* making the bed and sweeping the tile floor who were inside. Not John.

It was late afternoon before Ed gave up and walked back to the Rosarito, his heart heavy. He went up the flight of stairs to his room and inside flung himself on the bed. He was exhausted, drained from the emotional train derailing in his psyche. Was it over? It was too soon, because he wasn't ready. Usually there were warning signs, but this was so sudden. He knew he had no right to assume that John had equally strong feelings for him. Nothing had been said, but they had been inseparable for weeks. Now John was gone all day without a word. Where???

His thoughts were interrupted by a banging on the door to his room. He got up and opened the door. John was there in the doorway and strode into his room out of breath. "Have you already had dinner? I want to take you to dinner. Then he told Ed how Emmet and Frankie had popped in early and whisked him away to Manzanillo in Emmet's car. "They wouldn't take no for an answer. But we stopped in some really cool places, Indian markets, some ruins called Juxetepec. We had oysters in Barra de Navidad at a beach restaurant where the water rides right up into the restaurant and washes over your feet."

Ed was so happy to see John he barely heard John's narrative of the day's events. "And you don't have to worry about Frankie. There was no hanky panky. Emmet keeps him on a tight leash when he isn't drinking." Ed put his arms around John and stopped his story with a kiss, tasting the lips he had hungered for the entire day.

"Fuck Frankie!" he said and kissed John again. John let himself be led to the bed and stripped of his clothes. He let Ed ravage him and responded with enough ardor to relieve Ed of his anxiety. They went to dinner at Paco's and sat intimately under the tiki torches, partially hidden by large leafy plants. "Where do we go from here?" Ed asked.

John knew what he meant but pretended he didn't. "Go where?"

"Is there an *us?*"

"I think so," was John's inadequate reply.

"You know I'm crazy about you, Baby. You know that don't you?"

A trapped look flashed across John's face, but he quickly recovered. "I like you too, but I leave in four days for Houston. What then?"

Ed dropped his head in his hands. "I don't know. I've tried not to think about it." John didn't seem to have anything to offer; so Ed continued. "Can't you stay a little longer; just until I figure things out?"

"How can I? If I'm not on that flight I lose my job. I'm already in the doghouse because I blew the negotiations."

"They're not signing?"

"Oh, they're signing alright but on their terms."

"What happened?"

"Let's just say I was distracted. My boss is less than thrilled. So I've got to get back and face the music." Ed tried to picture himself in Houston, playing the little wife to John's corporate self, the person he knew John would change back into as soon as he traded floral shirts and *hauraches* for tailor-made suits and Florsheim shoes. Ed already knew this infatuation would have to end. Its inevitable conclusion was written into the circumstances of their meeting. The only question was whether he could end it gracefully.

They left Paco's and walked down the beach, strolling along the water's edge on the hard, wet sand. It was dark and they held hands as they walked. The tide brought the briny surf in to lap at their toes. The moon, hidden by clouds, began to shine on the water as the clouds blew apart by a sudden evening breeze. The tropical night was both romantic and poignant as they idled along, silently thinking and not thinking of their imminent parting.

"Will you think of me from time to time?" John finally asked.

"Are you kidding?" Ed replied. "I won't be able to stop thinking about you for a long time."

"What are you going to do?" John wondered aloud. "You never said."

"I don't know. Stay here for awhile. Try to patch it up with Emmet and Frankie. I must admit I'm a little spoiled by the Molina. It's not going to be easy going back to the Rosarito."

"Admit it," said John. "You miss *las cucarachas*."

Ed gave John a little affectionate punch on the arm. "I'll miss you. That's what I'll miss. I miss you already, and you haven't left yet."

"Come to Houston. Take a vacation."

"What do you think this is? I'm not exactly a man of leisure. I've got to get back to work while I still have some."

Reality had dawned upon both of them. It was as if the curtain fell on a lovely romance, and when the curtain rose again they would be far apart and immersed in the daily routines of real life. What had passed was not real, and they both knew it. Walking on the malecon they stopped and sat on a bench for awhile not talking. They were both restraining themselves from using the word "love". The fear of rejection lurked just out of mind.

Finally John said "Do you think the truest love remains unspoken?"

Ed wondered what he meant. He pondered the words over and over unable to answer. Was John questioning whether they were in love? He knew he was, which was why he lost the words to respond. Perhaps everything hung on the right answer.

John, on the other hand, questioned his own feelings. He had never felt this way. Even with Cory it was another story. With Ed it was overwhelmingly intense. There had been someone once, Stamos, but that was another lifetime.

He couldn't stand the idea of being apart, and yet he was leaving, and they might never meet again (in all probability wouldn't). So this was really good-bye. Yet John was unable to get his mind off a troubling situation at home, which now that he faced the reality of his impending departure he needed to mentally cope. Any response from Ed would be a distraction.

So he very abruptly ended the conversation with an enigmatic "I guess I'm going to find out tomorrow," which was not in answer to anything Ed had said but only the result of his own mental ramble. It left poor Ed more confused than ever. They kissed goodnight at John's door, but before Ed could turn and walk away John pulled him inside and closed the door.

CHAPTER 7

Ed

Ed drove John to the airport, the reality of John's departure felt like a lead ball in the pit of his stomach. They chatted about inconsequential things as they rolled past flat green fields puddled with water from the last night's rain. In the terminal they put John's carry on bag on the shiny wooden bench and stood close to one another. They were silent; there was nothing to say now. The dreaded moment was at hand. There was nothing left except a final embrace when John's flight was announced. They touched lips and John was gone. Just like that it was over.

Back at the Rosarito Ed blindly began stuffing his bag with the few personal belongings he traveled with. He knew he had to get out. Puerto Vallarta would be unbearable without John. Fully packed, he sat on the bed and looked out the window. Dark clouds had moved in, turning the sky gray, further dampening his mood. It would rain soon, beautiful to look at but nasty to drive in. He should get going, but he continued to sit there, his mind turning over and over the events of the last few weeks. He wondered how he had gotten to the age of forty and still had no one in his life. John was wonderful but no more real than a mirage. Maybe he was looking for something that didn't exist. Maybe relationships were not meant to last. Ed felt hollow; a wind whipping up outside seemed to whistle through him.

These musings did nothing to lessen Ed's loneliness. He thought of Emmet, the one person Ed had loved most consistently through the years. There would always be Emmet, but now there was Frankie. Ed was almost amused to think one thought could banish another. It was as if there were two minds inside his head, playing some sort of high stakes game of oneupmanship. Emmet could be his salvation, someone worth his dedication. But there was Frankie. Ed felt something close to hatred. He couldn't bear to see Emmet in the clutches of a monster. It was time to get out of Vallarta.

He dropped down to the lobby and used their phone to call Carlos in Guadalajara. "Let's boogie," said Ed.

Carlos' voice came out raspy through the bad connection. "Too soon, Amigo. I still have people to see, *y mi madre es enferma.*

A sick mother. Just my luck. Nothing is going my way on this trip. He would have to go it alone on the long boring drive up the West Coast of Mexico. Carlos would fly back in a few weeks, but there was no way that Ed could wait.. He checked out of the Rosarito and put his bag in his car. He would have to stop at Emmet and Frankie's to say good-bye. If he left without a send off Emmet would blame himself, thinking he had done something to hurt or offend Ed. He couldn't allow that. He found a parking spot right beneath their balcony and knocked on their red lacquered door. Emmet answered the door and drew Ed inside. Frankie was sunning naked on the terrace and waved at Ed when he saw him. He turned on his back, offering Ed the full frontal view, but Ed felt only disgust.

Ed accepted a coffee and told Emmet of his plans for the drive. "I'm hoping to get to San Blas tonight and then spend tomorrow night in Guaymas." Frankie got up, came inside and strutted slowly past Ed, like a fashion model on a runway, before going into the bedroom to get dressed. He came out dressed in shorts and t-shirt and went out the front door, closing it behind him. Ed glanced at Emmet who shrugged, the look on his face saying more than words. "You've got to get out from under, Emmet. Can't you see what he's doing to you? I hate leaving you behind with him. I feel like I'm deserting you."

"You shouldn't worry about me, Ed. I'm a big boy."

"Drop him, Emmet, before it's impossible or too expensive."

Meanwhile outside Frankie taped a cello bag of marijuana to the underside of the fender covering the right front wheel of Ed's Volvo. Frankie's resentments controlled him. If someone betrayed or rejected or insulted him that person would have to be punished. At this moment he was punishing Ed for rejecting him and for talking trash to Emmet about him. He didn't actually know what Ed was saying, but he suspected it, and that was enough. He double checked to be sure the bag wasn't visible without close inspection. It would be a waste of pot if Ed found it himself. He also enjoyed the fact that sober alcoholic and oh so squeaky clean Ed would be carrying a whole lot of trouble under his fender. He smiled as he went back in the house. It was the most satisfying thing he had done all day.

CHAPTER 8

Frankie

Frankie was born in Kingsburg, a small town in Central California between Fresno and Visalia, halfway on the road to nowhere folks used to say. His high school was at least an hour away, and so was the Dairy Queen where the "cool" kids hung out. Not that Frankie could ever have been mistaken as a "cool" kid. He was more likely to have worked there than hung out there. His small stature eliminated him from most sports. He could swim but football was king in Kingsburg, and a swimmer was nobody. His tan skin inherited from some long ago Mexican ancestor made him an outsider and a victim of occasional abuse. He was the sort of boy other boys liked to beat up on. He was pretty nimble, but he couldn't always avoid it. Frankie knew he was queer from the time he was eight, when Monk, Carla, his older sister's boyfriend, molested him. It happened frequently enough that Frankie decided he liked it. When Carla and Monk broke up Frankie started going out looking for it. Sometimes boys hung out in front of Uncle Bob's Used Cars under the strands of bright lights illuminating shiny Fords, Chevrolets. GMC pickups, and male packages ready to drive right off the lot.

Frankie lusted for a pickup, like the one cool kid Jimmy Blunt drove that had camouflage painted doors and flew a Confederate flag from its antenna. But Frankie couldn't hold a job. He had a habit of speaking his mind which was usually filled with bitterness. He gained precious little money from the occasional tips he received for giving blow jobs at the highway rest stop. He dropped out of high school in the tenth grade, sick of the bullies that hung him upside down in the gymnasium from the still rings. When Carla moved to San Diego to be near her boyfriend, Slade, who was stationed at Camp Pendleton, claiming she always had a thing for a Marine, Frankie moved with her.

Carla and Frankie had been raised by their single mom, Corinne, who one night staggered out of the Ole Lamplighter bar in Visalia and drove her battered old Buick into Horseshoe Gulch which drops off thirty feet into a rusty car littered ravine. Carla worked at the Dairy Queen and The Dollar Store and managed to buy groceries out of her meager earnings. She had her fair share of boyfriends who would usually fork over the rent on their tiny two room apartment over the 24 Hour Gas Station in Kingsburg which was also a hangout after the Dairy Queen closed at ten.

Frankie knew there had to be better places than this dusty rural backwater. He dreamed of big city life. He had heard stories of gay bars crammed with gay men looking for sex. He was told tales of great parks where strapping dudes with giant dicks lurked behind every bush. When they arrived in San Diego Frankie set out immediately to find and be found. But Frankie had no idea where to look for this dreamy scene. Even if he found the bars he was too young to go inside. He was only sixteen. He had heard of Balboa Park, and he took two buses to get there. He hung out in the various gardens, but only straight people wandered through, sometimes in droves. Sometimes a couple of men holding hands would pass by, but Frankie didn't know how to approach them.

Then one day he met Carter Winthrop. Carter was in his mid-sixties and had once been handsome, but too many martinis and a thousand tricks had left him with eye bags and sagging jowls. Frankie wouldn't have given a second glance, but he was desperate. Carter noticed Frankie first and followed him at a discreet distance from the zoo to the San Diego Air and Space Museum from which he had been driven by a scowling attendant after he tried to sneak in. He was sitting on the curb, dejected, when Carter approached him. "You want to go inside. I'll take you. I saw that guard. He wasn't very nice."

"Fuck him!" was Frankie's sullen response. But he was looking Carter over, sizing and summing him up. He didn't see Carter in terms of sex at all, but he might be good for a meal. He hadn't eaten at all since the day before. "I'm hungry. Do you know where they serve food around here?" He knew but this was how he got right to the point. They had burgers at the Blue Panda, and Frankie ordered large fries and a milk shake. Carter willingly sprang for all the food that Frankie could eat. He was used to boys demanding much more expensive places to dine.

Carter was just the sort of mark Frankie had been waiting for, although he wouldn't have phrased it in urban street slang. Daddy would be more like it. Since Frankie had grown up without a father he may have been seeking one, but only one he could manipulate. He had no use for sort of father that would artfully guide him into a self-reliant manhood. He didn't need one for that. He had already noted his assets, and he knew what they could get him. Carter was more than willing to be a daddy. He saw it as a last chance for lust before succumbing to a withered old age. He courted Frankie like he was a virginal maiden, showering him with gifts and squiring him about in regal fashion with an expensive wardrobe unfortunately flaunted by someone without a clue as to how to wear it. They were the year's odd couple. As soon as he could Carter moved Frankie into his craftsman bungalow on High Street, but housekeeping was entirely new to Frankie and an anathema as well. Frankie, who was inherently lazy, would not lift a finger. Articles of clothing remained in the place where he had removed them. Cigarette butts piled up in ashtrays in every room, and sometimes were found in objects never designed for charred tobacco. Tennis shoes appeared inexplicably in the dining room. Wet towels covered the floor of the bathroom and sometimes made their way into the bedroom. The cleaning lady gave her notice, and Carter ran about like a mad hen picking up after Frankie, emptying ashtrays, becoming for all intents and purposes Frankie's personal maid. For a man as anal as Carter this was unbearable. Was fabulous sex worth it? Maybe. But the little sex that Frankie doled out to Carter clearly wasn't. It wouldn't take much to push him over the edge. Carter even resorted to bribery. Frankie had no access to drugs except through Carter. Even if he had the contacts to score he didn't have the cash to pay for drugs. By doling out marijuana Carter was able for a time to minimize the mess. Ridding the living room of cum stained underpants cost him three joints. Five joints would buy him clean ashtrays for a two days. An ounce of his own got the lawn mowed. There was bound to be a point at which Carter had enough, but most of his friends were surprised it took several years to come. That day came when Frankie dropped the Ming vase while trying to hide the ounce of pot that Carter thought was so cleverly hidden in the floor model radio/record player.. Frankie left no cushion unturned, no sweater still hanging, no drawer not emptied in his desperate search until he found it inside the antique cuckoo clock. In his haste to transfer it from Carter's hiding place to one of his own he dropped the vase and watched it shatter on the gleaming hardwood floor. Upon hearing the noise Carter came running from the kitchen where he had been washing

Frankie's breakfast dishes. There, scattered on the floor, were a multitude of pieces which had formerly comprised his priceless vase. As the realization dawned, a shock wave flooded his entire being and he turned beet red and began to scream and yell, even throwing furniture at Frankie, in fact becoming completely unhinged. Frankie must have realized that he was losing a particularly nice set up by being a slob and thinking Carter would put up with it forever. He must have known he had blown it when he found himself locked out of the house, and his meager belongings scattered over Carter's spacious lawn. He called his sister only to discover the number disconnected, and there was no new number.

There followed days of despair as Frankie wandered about with no idea where his next meal would come from let alone a roof over his head. He tried social services by pretending he was an alcoholic and found shelter in a halfway house, but that lasted only one night after he was caught smoking the bent joint he had stashed in his shoe. He joined some other kids who slept in an empty warehouse with the rats and roaches. He didn't have a sleeping bag or blanket like the others, and sleeping on cold concrete was murder. Besides the other kids didn't like him. They thought him a smart ass and were beyond impervious to his charms. He spent many cold and hungry nights and resorted to stealing to survive.

Frankie met a kid called Froggie outside Nellie's where the nightly drag shows attracted a lot of well off gay men. The competition among these young hanging about hustlers was stiff. The best thing Frankie had going was underage.

It was the extra little charge a daddy could get from breaking the law. Froggie introduced him to Arnie Dodger, who looked right out of Dickens and could easily have been a pal of Oliver Twist, and who thought he could somehow make a buck off Frankie. He cleaned him up, bought him some clothes, taught him how to walk and talk, and fucked him good too. It was for Frankie definitely an education. And that was how he met Calvin Clement who threw the best parties and knew all the best people. And it was at one of those posh parties that the newly butched up Frankie met Emmet Stone.

CHAPTER 9

Emmet

Emmet Stone began writing plays and stories in high school in his English class encouraged by his teacher, Elizabeth Warden, a single, still not spinsterish young woman, who most of the teen boys in the class lusted after. However, they were to Elizabeth with the exception of Emmet, young Neanderthals, grunting and pawing at each other, stealing homework, cheating on tests. But not Emmet. Instead, he wrote her a sonnet entitled *Ode to an Eponymous Rose, thy name is Elizabeth*.

Since he was in Liz' English class and also belonged to the drama club it was inevitable that Liz would invite him to write the annual Christmas play. It would be timely to mention that Emmet did not call or refer to Elizabeth as Liz. That was an invention of the Cro-Magnon football squad that sat in the rear of the class and made fart sounds with their armpits.

It was inevitable that Emmet, who carried himself with an attitude of superiority, would attract the attention of school bullies. They laid in wait for him in hallways, locker rooms and the cafeteria. Walking with his tray he had to be alert for the sudden leg that shoots into his path. Locker rooms were particularly dangerous because Emmet, in spite of his better judgment, could not help admiring the young male bodies that surrounded him. More than once he was slammed into his locker and came out with a broken nose. Once, walking home along Delong Street, a car braked in front of him and four boys jumped out and shoved him to the ground. They quickly stripped him naked, and then made fun of his body. "Ew! He's soft and white and fat. He's disgusting." Then, grabbing all his clothes, they drove away laughing. Emmet finished walking home with a garbage can lid concealing his privates.

All in all high school was hell for Emmet, but he got his revenge with the Christmas play, creating characters which closely resembled his tormentors and writing them as the louts they were. As he was also directing, he cast some of the boys to play themselves, knowing they were too dimwitted to recognize that fact. The high level of buffoonery in the play made it a huge success with the school as a whole, and Emmet wrote and directed several more plays before he graduated. It was inevitable that Emmet would find his way to Hillcrest and become part of the gay scene there. Finally in his element, he thrived among the thronging bars and wild clubs. It was a different trick he dragged home every night. "Better than a butcher shop," he claimed. "Fresh meat every night." He was surrounded by genuine admirers and wannabe groupies, who wished to share a bit of Emmet's limelight. He was a strict enough disciplinarian to not let his love life interfere with his writing or was it the other way around? When one or the other seemed threatened he adroitly combined them. His popularity in the gay scene quickly led to invitations to write plays for local theater groups. He quickly rose through the ranks until he was invited to write a play for HEP, Hillcrest Equity Players, the crème de la crème of community theater, an organization with unionized actors and featuring plays by almost known playwrights, the up and coming type, long hair, scruffily dressed but very handy with the words. And Emmet was one of them.

It was during the staging of his third play, *Winter's Remorse*, that a young set designer, presented his portfolio to Harmon Starcase for perusal. Harmon was equivical. "I don't know," he said to anyone within hearing, but especially to Ed, the young man with the portfolio. "The drawings are very good, but I don't think the design is what we're looking for."

Emmet, who had already had more than a glimpse of Ed and found him to be exactly what he was looking for, danced in and said, "Well, let Mother have a lookie poo," upon which he minced across the room and snatched them from Harmon's clutches almost as if he had been admiring the crown jewels just a little too long.

"Marveloso! Absolutely marveloso! This staircase is perfect for my entrance in the second act. And those windows. They are just the sort of windows that Sir Henry could wistfully gaze through for the entire dreadful winter while pining for the Duchess Margaretta who's been abroad for the entire season. Harmon must you be a complete boor and an utter philistine? These are just perfect, my dear. And what was your name again, handsome?"

That was how Ed got to be the set designer (and builder and decorator and general factotum) for Hillcrest Equity Players. Emmet could be very sweet, especially when he was telling Ed how he liked his coffee, "black with just the merest hint of honey. Just wave the jar over it. Just the way you wave the vermouth over my martini. Isn't he sweet" he would say to others "and divinely handsome? I've only glimpsed the crown jewels but I can tell you they could serve as a king's ransom." At this point he would fan himself vigorously in case anyone didn't quite get it.

It was not long before Emmet found reasons to stay late at the theater when most of the set construction was occurring.

He would grab some young twat or other and read lines or sometimes recite an entire speech. If the boy (it was always a boy) was cute enough he would say "Darling, you were divine. You should be in the show. Can I offer you a drink? Oh, it's past your bedtime. Well, run along home. Mama would love to tuck you in some other time." Those young stage hands couldn't compete with the adorableness of young twenty-two year old Ed, a recent college boy with striking looks and an attitude of shy sincerity and very interesting designs, settings that Emmet could picture himself inside.

Ed was intrigued with Emmet, partially because he knew who he was and partially because he thought he could learn a few things, which he did, but they were not the things he thought they would be. Still, he had never met anyone like Emmet and, if truth be told, would never again, because Emmet was a thing unto himself, an avatar, an apotheosis of the theatrical personality. And when the light beamed from this virtual lighthouse it illuminated Ed's entire world. Such was the adeptness of a courting Emmet that the light shined for Ed alone.

They lived together for several years, and it was the best time of Ed's life. He had a lover that he was crazy about. Emmet was his first, and he remained almost virginal for sometime, because sex with Emmet was a chancy thing. You had to catch him between bar tricks and diddled stage cuties. Young actors were his specialty, and he parlayed his reputation, a mixture of celebre du theatre and horny goat which had some of those cuties on the run. Ed was completely wowed. After four years of college and a year and a half at a dead end unrelated job he was more than ready to find his calling, and at Hillcrest Equity players with an in house bona fide mentor he believed he had found it.

But after the first couple of years playing house with a man of the house that was more absent than present he naturally began to feel neglected. He didn't so much object to holding Emmet's head while he vomited his three martini dinner or dragging him away from mid flirtation, but the many long nights, when Emmet didn't come home at all or came home with some young honey cooing and wooing as they tumbled together in Ed and Emmet's bedroom behind a shut and locked door finally got to him. One day he gathered the clothes that he had moved in with and a couple of birthday gifts from Emmet and moved out and into the apartment of one of the actor's in the show, Darby, and Emmet came home to an empty apartment.

All Emmet could say was "She'll be back." But that didn't happen. Ed was crushed and resigned from the company to become a freelance designer and closed the book on the Emmet chapter of his life. But he never really got over him.

Instead his passion morphed into a motherly caring, contenting himself to watching over the irascible Emmet.

CHAPTER 10

John's Lament

When Ed left John at the *aeropuerto* he was in line to board. Ed had left, and he was despondent. Then there came an announcement over the PA in Spanish with static. *Flight 797 from Puerto Vallarta to Houston, Texas is delayed because of damage to the aircraft. Another plane is being brought over from Guadalajara.* It might be hours, giving him more time to think, something he didn't really want to do. He longed to just put his arms around Ed and hold him, something he would never do again. It all seemed so final. He was sure he had never felt this way about another person. He was leaning with his back against the wall of the terminal, and suddenly his legs buckled, and he slid down until he was sitting on the shiny floor, tears streaming down his face. He had never done this before, but he didn't care who saw him. If anyone did they paid no attention.

This was not John's first affair. There has been others, and the parting was not emotional. In fact most of the time it was long overdue. This one was different. He had never felt this way before. John knew he was attractive with his mop of wavy black hair, lake blue eyes and Hollywood lips. Both women and men hit on him, and some of the men were straight. John took most of those advances in stride, but when Ed spoke to him at the meeting he melted. He loved the soft, husky quality of his voice, which, even when he spoke up, sounded quiet. He liked the strong sun browned hand that shook his own. The slight, quizzical look over John's stumbling words made him smile, remembering. He was taken right from the first word Ed spoke to him. John thought about Cory. He should call and let him know his ETA. He hadn't thought about Cory in weeks, and now he couldn't stop thinking about Ed.

He thought about their lovemaking. The quaking climaxes, the long shudders to spent satisfaction. He thought of places they visited together, cafes they hung out in, hikes through the ever thick and humid jungles. He admired the little houses that Ed loved so much. *La casa bonita!* Ed would say, blowing it a kiss. He adored swimming in the rapid river with Ed and watching the water go over the lip of the fall. He enjoyed everything they did together, and now they would never do anything together again. This reality came thundering home like a bolt of lightening. The reality he had fervently avoided could no longer be avoided. The truth was that he would probably not. He would never see Ed again. This brought more tears. His mind began to catalog things not done with Ed: They had never rode horses together or gone mountain climbing. He wanted to see Yosemite with Ed and the Grand Canyon and the giant Sequoias that Ed had so lovingly described. Now he never would. He thought of Ed's flat hard chest and the warm legs that has so recently clasped him. He thought of Ed's wiry biceps, and remembered how strong he was. How he was able to hold him tight while the river's current tried to pull them over the falls. He said to Ed "Don't let me go". It was then that Ed whispered in his ear. "I could never let you go." And yet he had.

CHAPTER 11

The Drive

By the time Ed rolled out of Puerto Vallarta it was noon. No way was he going to make Mazatlan before dark, when driving in Mexico becomes too hazardous to justify the distance achieved. If he pushed it he might make San Blas, forgetting the cloud of suspicion that he might be under surrounding the theft of the Egyptian dagger.

The air was still and humid when Ed left the highway and took the turn off to San Blas. The vegetation was thick and tangled on both sides of the road. He passed a small meadow where egrets were making their rookery among the palmettos and moss laden oaks while bat falcons flapped among the tree tops. He even spotted a heron swooping over rivulets to find its dinner between smooth stones. Another time Ed might have parked and wandered through swampy glades, but now his only thought was to put Mexico behind him.

It was almost dark when he reached San Blas. He checked into the hotel, changed clothes in his room and dropped down to the bar. The bartender seemed to recognize him and brought him a gin and tonic before he ordered. "Welcome back," he said, setting the chilled glass in front of Ed. "Ed, right?"

"Yes, but I don't remember your name."

"It's a skill that takes practice to develop. Sometimes your tips depend upon it."

Ed took his drink and wandered onto the terrace where a foursome were playing some card game that included whoops and cackles. The bar itself was empty save for one couple at a table in the corner, who were wrapped in their own intimate privacy. He settled in a chair to watch the last lingering rays of sunlight paint the deck and the gardens between the hotel and the little beach a rosy hue. An ivory billed woodpecker began his echoed knocking while *chachalacas* flitted in the bromeliad patch. Only a few years back he had been an active birder, and these spottings would have given him a few thrills, but now he could no longer be bothered to find his notebook and jot a description. The past few weeks lay on him like a heavy stone.

John drifted back into his mind, and he wondered when he would stop thinking about him. Distance had somewhat dulled the ache he felt from the moment they parted. John was gone, far away, in a distant place, absorbed back into a life that held no place for Ed. He knew he must forget all about him, make him no more than a fond memory. He tried to think of the work waiting for him in Hillcrest, his apartment with the plants Doretta had promised to water, things he had planned to do before he left, like bike to La Jolla with Gary, but those thoughts seemed to belong to another time, almost another life. Thoughts of John inevitably came flooding back.

Wrapped up in these thoughts he didn't notice the bartender making a phone call. The card players finished their game and retired to the dining room, and suddenly it was too quiet in the almost deserted bar. The bartender erased the gloom of dusk by turning on lights, and Ed ordered another drink. He had two more before he stumbled up to his room.

He lay on the bed in the dark without undressing. He thought about Frankie. What was there about him that was so unlikable? He was cordial, friendly, you could say even gracious. He was sure he couldn't be trusted. He disliked him from the start, and yet it went beyond untrustworthy. Even before Frankie tried to put the make on him, he saw something mean in Frankie, a streak that he tried to keep hidden, but Ed had glimpsed it while Frankie was unaware he was being watched. Ed's intuition told him to be wary of this kid. Don't get on his bad side. He wondered if his rejection of Frankie had been too brusque.

When the room stopped spinning Ed fell asleep only to be troubled by anxiety filled dreams, one fragment containing a moving car full of laughing people, a man demanding Ed's shirt and from nowhere Ed's father looking for his fedora. Finally before he awoke he was naked in a cornfield, and there were snakes you couldn't see because of the thick vegetation on the ground. He proceeded carefully because he knew they were there but he never saw them. He woke more tired than he was the night before, but having drank dinner he was hungry and had a decent breakfast before getting back on the road.

It was late morning and Ed was driving fast, hoping to make Mazatlan in time to catch the ferry that left at 4pm. When he saw in his rear view mirror the flashing blue and red lights of a Mexican patrol car his hopes sank. He pulled over. "Good morning, Officer," he said, when he saw the familiar face of the man, dressed in brown striding up to the driver side door.

"We meet again," said Lt. Hernan Cortes Rodriguez. "It is such a pleasure to meet an old friend on this lonely highway. Driving up and down with no one to talk to. Perhaps if I had a partner..." he trailed off. "but this is a poor country, and in such a poor country companionship is not provided by the government. One man is expected to do the work of several."

"A pleasure to see you again, Lieutenant. I can save you some time. I still have no *armas*."

"Time is all I have, my friend. Please, if you would step out of the car." Ed got out of the car and placed his hands on the roof while Rodriguez did his pat down. "You see *armas* is not all we have to how you say look out for. These days everyone wants *drogas*. Bad men try to bring it to the *Estados Unidos*. Your *presidente* is very angry and yells at my *presidente* who then gets very angry and yells at me. Not to my face, *naturalmente*, but to my superiors who in turn yell at me. So what can I do? I have to be on the lookout for." Rodriguez finished his pat down, and then moved to inspect the car, looking in the glove box and under the front seat. He lifted Ed's duffel and dumped the content on the back seat. Having completed his examination of the interior, he stepped out and began looking under the car, finally arriving at the right front fender. He did not say anything for a few minutes or even touch the bag of marijuana taped to the underside of the fender. He stood up, returned to his vehicle and said something in Spanish into his CB radio. Ed was puzzled but Rodriguez ignored him. Presently another car arrived, and the two officers escorted Ed to the back seat of the new officer's car. Rodriguez put on gloves and removed the bag of marijuana in the presence of the other officers and placed the bag in a large plastic bag. Rodriguez got behind the wheel of Ed's car and followed the other car onto the highway.

After about an hour they pulled off the highway into a dusty little village, a few buildings, some houses, some cars, a market and not much else, not even a *zocalo*. Small half naked children played in the muddy street, and a ragged looking dog barked at the police cars as they passed. "Where are we?" asked Ed.

"Acaponeta. It's very small. You probably no hear of it. But why spend several more hours driving to Mazatlan when I know the judge I must see has left for the weekend? Here there is a judge who is *mi amigo. Comprende?*" For the first time a sense of foreboding came over Ed.

They went inside a squat building that looked like somebody's house. A woman was cooking in the kitchen and several children were sitting on the floor watching a black and white television. "¡Jorge!" Rodriguez called out. "¡*Ven aqui! Tenemos un cliente.*" A man appeared in the doorway of a bedroom. He was unshaven and wore dirty, baggy pants and an undershirt. He rubbed his eyes, still half asleep. Rodriguez held up the plastic bag with the ounce of marijuana in it. "¡*Mira! Mota!*"

"Maybe we could find a way to settle this without the formalities," said Ed, feeling around in his back pocket for his wallet.

"Looking for this?" asked Rodriguez. He held up Ed's billfold. "My apologies but it is *confiscado.*" Jorge, the bailiff, cleared a desk in the corner by pushing everything on it onto the floor. He took a notebook out of a drawer, opened it to a new form and began filling in blanks."

"¿*Nombre?*"

"Edward Martin. M-a-r-t-i-n."

"¿*Nacionalidad?*"

"American."

At the completion of the interview the bailiff stamped the document with several stamps and filed it in a drawer, and Rodriguez ushered Ed to another building with bars on the one window. Ed was directed inside, and the door was closed and locked behind him. His eyes adjusted slowly to the dim interior lit only by a shaft of light entering through the dirty window. The floor was bare concrete and over in one corner sat a pail. There was no furniture in the room. The floor had not been mopped in what appeared to be months, and there were things crawling around on it that Ed could not identify. Ed lay down, not wanting to touch the walls that were slimy, something he'd discovered as soon as he leaned against it.

Ed's feelings were a mixture of horror and revulsion regarding his surroundings and anxiety concerning his future. They had taken his money, and he assumed his possessions were *confiscado*. He knew he had to figure out how to get through this. He did not feel he was in physical danger. They had treated him in a professional manner, although it was not the sort of professionalism to which he was accustomed. The last bit of light faded away, and he lay there in the dark, brushing away things that were crawling over him. He wanted to sleep, because he saw no reason to be awake. He wanted to sleep and then to awake and find it all over without dwelling on the thought that what was next might be worse.

Somehow, despite the discomfort and because the day's events had drained him of energy, he fell into a troubled sleep, waking and not knowing if he had slept hours or only a few seconds. His body ached from the cold hard floor, and his face on the concrete was wet from who knows what. He was startled wide awake by the sound of a key turning in a lock and the screeching of a metal door opening. It was dark outside but still lighter than inside, and Ed saw Rodriguez and several other uniformed officers framed in the doorway. "*Ven, amigo!* We are going to Guadalajara."

Ed found the back seat of a patrol car a huge step up in physical comfort, but the sense of foreboding continued to grow. His only hope was that big city procedures included accountability and safety of foreign persons. Nobody wanted the U.S. Embassy on their back. He did not fall back asleep, because they were driving through rugged mountainous country, and all the swerving around bends in the road was making him carsick. He forced the nausea down, knowing if he vomited on one of the officers it might result in physical recriminations. Instinctively he knew in these situations that not calling attention to oneself was the safest mode of conduct.

CHAPTER 12

Guadalajara

Ed gradually became aware that his destination was not another court. From his position in the back of the car he could see they were driving alongside high stone walls topped with razor wire. He could see nothing of the buildings beyond the wall, but from what he could interpret from the mutterings of his back seat companions, who were conversing in hushed tones, mostly in Spanish but lapsing into English occasionally for what he assumed was his benefit, he knew this was no backwoods lockup. This was the real deal, *Campo Muerte,* (as it was notoriously referred to), otherwise known as Jalisco Correctional Institution. He concluded that whatever pleas he had made to what he imagined were judges had been met with stony rejection. Now he was about to be shoved into the most infamous prison in all Mexico, and that his future existence, if there was even to be one, depended upon a resourcefulness that he was not sure he possessed.

Ed's life to this point had been a relatively easy one. As a boy with loving parents he had come to take the basics of living entirely for granted. As a teen he was primarily occupied with social status and sex, the latter discovered in a series of steps that avoided shame and castigation. By the time he was twenty he was a cog in a comfortable social wheel. Sex came and went and he ventured forth in the world to make his place based in no small part on his talents and social connections. He had no idea how he was to deal with this new world he was entering, but he told himself, I *can* do this."

They entered through a metal door in the stone wall. He was turned over to several uniformed guards, and his escorts bid him *adios,* one of them slapping his back and wishing him *buena suerte.* In the guard room off the entrance more papers were stamped, photographs taken, and Ed was made to remove every piece of clothing. An inspection was made of his body which Ed felt at times was unnecessarily thorough. The eye contact he made with one of the guards told him they would be seeing more of each other. Ed's mind immediately began working. This might be a good thing, something he could use to his advantage. How would having a guard in his camp affect his standing with the inmate population? That, he imagined, he would soon find out.

They went from the guard room down a long hallway with what appeared to be offices on either side and through another door which took them outside, a large area enclosed by prison walls in which hundreds of men milled about, most in groups, both large and small. Some had charcoal grills and were preparing food, others played cards or gambled with dice, many smoked. They wore their own clothing. Only the guards wore uniforms. There were half a dozen tents in the yard, the purpose of which aroused Ed's curiosity. As they crossed the yard many eyes were upon him, and Ed did his best to retain an expression of disinterest.

Back inside the building Ed realized they were now in a cell block. Many inmates were outside, but there were plenty in the cells as well. Ed counted about six beds in each cell. As if he read Ed's mind, the guard escorting him, whose name was

Alvaro, said, "Is many staying here, *mucho gente,* maybe *veinte* in cell. If you want bed you pay." They stopped at a cell with two men sleeping inside.

"More outside," Alvaro said and gave Ed a pat on the butt as he pushed him inside. Another guard following close behind tossed Ed's duffel in with him. Ed was happy to see it again and even happier when he found his confiscated money inside. One of the inmates sat up awakened by the loud crash clank of the metal door closing.

"And you are who?" the man said. He was white and sounded American. The sleeping man had dark skin, most likely Mexican, maybe indigenous.

"I'm Ed."

"You got a smoke?"

"I don't. It's a nasty habit and hard to quit."

"That's too bad. Cigarettes are like gold here." The man said. "Everybody smokes. There ain't nothing else to do. If something else don't kill you first other people's smoke will." He coughed twice, proving his point. "My name's Miller, but they call me The Shrimp, *La Camaron.* He was small, fleshy and balding, about fifty, had a mustache and eye bags the size of saucers. "I ain't pretty but I got a great butt. You'll see it soon. It makes me popular with the men. Sleeping beauty over there they call Colombo. These aren't our beds. When the others come back we get back up. This bed belongs to Marco. I do him favors, and he lets me use it when he's not in it. You could call it a rental.

"So what you in for? Drugs, I bet. Seventy-five percent of the inmates are in here for drugs. The rest are in for rape or murder. This is a business, chum, a business that couldn't exist without illegal drugs. But it's an excuse for the Gove to take what it wants, and the fool taxpayers pay by the inmate. It's the most profitable racket in the whole damn country."

The sound of approaching voices told Ed the recreation period was over. He could hear cells opening and closing on the floor below. Then he heard them on his floor, including the one he was in. A half dozen men filed into the cell, the door of which clanged shut behind them. As they took their accustomed places several noticed Ed crouching in the corner, and one said, "Looks like we got the newbie." Ed ignored him and inspected his duffel. Some of his clothes were missing, and with his back to the others he counted his money. That was light too. Ed wondered why any of it was still there. Maybe they thought he would need it. In his bag was a change of underwear, a towel and a bar of soap. Ed wondered what he could use for a toothbrush.

The one called Fowler was saying, "The bullshit in the yard has to stop. They're going to cut our rations."

"They cut them anyway. They don't need no excuse."

"Shut up, Camaron. Nobody asked you." someone said.

"Let's call a meeting," said Fowler.

"Let's wait. I say we deal with Trevino first," someone else jumped in. "He's the one always starts the trouble."

"What happened?" Miller wanted to know.

"Someone pulled a knife and Trevino took it away. The guards didn't even see it," Rocky answered.

"Now Trevino has a knife. That's not good."

"But at least we know it. Just don't let him start something with you."

Alvarro stopped outside the cell. "Hey, Camaron. Put on something pretty. La Cucaracha wants to see you." Miller made a little show of stripping while he put on a pair of tight, white shorts. A mod wig made him look ten years younger.

Fowler grunted. "If you'd shave off that damn mustache I'd fuck you myself." He finally noticed Ed and beckoned him with a crooked finger. Ed walked over and joined his circle. "You must be Ed. Your name came up in the scuttlebutt this morning. I'm Fowler. I sort of run this cell. I've got one rule: You don't make trouble for me; I don't make trouble for you."

"I don't make trouble for anyone," Ed said placidly.

"That's a very good answer. We sometimes get these guys who like to show off. Right away I can see they're going to be trouble. The guards like us. They think we're on their side. Let's keep it that way."

Right away Ed could tell that Fowler liked him, not in a sexual way, although that couldn't be ruled out. They were about the same age, lean men in fairly good shape. It was a matching of intellect that was apparent from the start. Fowler knew instinctively he could talk to Ed, exchange theories, talk strategy, maybe even plan an escape with him. They could be co-managers. They did talk, whispering late into the night. Fowler leaned into Ed, talking softly in his ear. "Most of these yahoos don't know their ass from a horses rectum. I could tell right off you were smart. You're someone I can tell stuff to and know it won't be blabbed. I feel I can trust you, but before I do I have to test you." Ed said nothing, waiting for Fowler to continue.

"Basically we've got a good bunch of men in this cell. I've managed to weed out the bad apples, but I sense there's still someone that can't be trusted. I want you to find out who it is. Get to know them, gain their confidence, encourage them to spill their guts. Be their father confessor."

Ed laughed. "Do I look like a priest?"

"You know what I mean. I'll be watching. I want to believe in you."

Ed knew that while he was reviewing them they would be reviewing him. It was the prison vetting system. If he was to be Fowler's lieutenant a number of men would have to sign off on the deal. In addition to Fowler and Miller actual cell mates included Humphrey Bowles, a used car salesman from Temple, Texas, who went to a bachelor party in Matamoros and ended up in a drunken brawl in Ciudad Victoria. How he got there or how he came to drive the mayor's car through a plate glass window he had no idea. He wasn't so much pissed off that he was in jail as he was that his buddies were in a nicer cell block. "That's the breaks, Bowles," was Fowler's comment. "Now quit your bleeding."

El Hongo, the mushroom, was actually shaped like one, big head, thick neck, scrawny body. Once in the cell he seldom moved from any spot he occupied. Tommy The Toad was the living example of wrack and ruin. He had been in prison for ten years, having murdered a man in the course of turning a trick. He claimed self-defense, but the broken beer bottle in the dead man's hand did not convince the jury. Back then he was Tommy The Twink and everybody's fuckpiece on the block. But time had not been kind to Tommy and by the time he was forty he was so ugly he couldn't even buy sex. Then there were the Mexican twins, Javier and Jose, good looking boys in their thirties whose only company was each other. They spoke little English, and, although they were never seen engaging in acts of incest, the consensus was they were lovers. "Why would they fuck anyone else?" was Fowler's opinion.

There were half a dozen temps. Throw in hangers on and Fowler's posse and the cell was always packed. There was a never ending card game on one of the beds, which someone named Julio rented out. No one had ever seen this Julio who it was rumored spent all his time with a boyfriend in Cell Block Three. All business in the prison was conducted through intermediaries. You never knew whom you're really buying from or selling to. Ed knew that Fowler had clout and knew how to use it. He concluded that Fowler taking a liking to him was the first good thing to happen on this whole rotten fucking trip.

CHAPTER 13

Cellular Life

Ed was allowed to write a check on his bank in San Diego. "We know where you live," was Alvaro's remark which he followed up with a handful of Ed's butt. "If you'd be nicer you wouldn't have to sleep on a concrete floor. I've got a *primo* room in one of those *casitas* in the yard. I got it fixed up real nice."

Ed just rolled his eyes. "Don't you ever quit?"

"Not when I see something I really like," said Alvaro, unzipping Ed's jump suit and running his hand over Ed's bare, hard body inside. "And I really like you."

Ed pulled away. "I'm not going to lead you on. I'm not interested."

This was probably Alvaro's dozenth rejection from Ed alone. Too bad Ed thought. He wasn't a bad looking guy, but Ed had sworn off sex for the time being. Otherwise he might have had a chance. Despite those rejections he took Ed to the cashier where he got a fistful of pesos which could buy him the amenities without which life in this prison would be unbearable. The exchange rate was terrible and gave him half as many pesos as he would have received on the outside. If he had to spend every penny he had, which wasn't that much, it would be worth it. No money was not an option that includes survival. Ed wondered how the poor Mexican made out until he realized that none of the inmates at *Campo Muerte* were dirt poor Mexicans. Most of the men had some resources; many were *gringos*. The system was not going to be bothered with imprisoning the *peon* whose usual crime was drunkenness. He was tossed back on the street in favor of those people who could pay out the heinie.

Eventually he was allowed to use Fowler's phone. It came with a warning that if confiscated Ed would pay with his left nut. In the laundry room Ed found a niche behind the dryers where no one would ever look because it's so blasted hot there your nipples fell off. Ed called Emmet, and his heart did a tap dance when he heard his voice.

"Where are you? We wondered why we hadn't heard from you."

"I'm in Jalisco Correctional."

"Campo Muerte? How in the Queen's titty did you get there?"

"It's a long story. Can you get me out?"

There was a pause. "How much money do you have?"

"None. *Nada. No hay.*"

"It's going to take more money than both of us have. I'll have to raise it. Give me some time. At least a week. You poor darling. If I could I'd rip the bars out to save your pretty ass, but I'm only a poor downtrodden ham who's watching his career fade before his very eyes."

"Cut the crap, Emmet. You should try spending even one night in here."

"Darling, being in prison is my favorite fantasy."

Ed ended the call just as two guards came into the room. They walked past where he was hiding, and he slipped out when they were talking in the far corner. When he told Fowler what was going to happen Fowler said "Maybe you can do something for me on the outside. I'll pay you $15,000, and you can pay your friend back." At first Ed wanted no part it, because anything that would pay that much had to be illegal. "No." It's perfectly legal. You would pick up a package in El Paso and deliver it in Houston. There's nothing illegal in the package, no drugs or guns, just some photograph's, nothing salacious, no children or animals. I swear on my grandmother's grave. I'm willing to make it worth your while because I need someone I can trust absolutely without question."

At first Ed wanted no part of whatever scheme Fowler proposed. Maybe Fowler could trust Ed, but could Ed trust Fowler? He's a con. He's in prison for Chrissake. How could he risk something as potentially dangerous as that? Was he willing to trade a Mexican prison for an American one? Suddenly everything got a lot more expensive. If one lousy ounce of pot could land you in *Campo Muerte,* think what the punishment would be for a $15,000 crime. But when Fowler mentioned Houston he started listening.

Since he had been in prison he thought constantly of John. Letting him go without plans to meet in the future was now the biggest mistake of his life. If he had been thinking at the time he could be snuggled with John now in some little nest in Houston and not in this filthy prison. Most of the men had relationships with other men in the prison, especially the Mexicans, and, when their wives came to visit it was one big happy family. *Gringos* were less likely to have male lovers, but there was no stigma to it. All the powerful guys, the *jefes,* had boyfriends that manipulated them, twisted them around their little pee pees. Ed yearned to be with John, in Houston or anywhere. What else did he have to think about? In the end he couldn't resist an opportunity that would take him to Houston, and the money waiting for him there would erase his debt to Emmet. How could he say no?

Emmet was waiting by the prison entrance the day they released him. Ed could not stop hugging him. "I'm always happy to see you, Emmet. But never more than today."

"Darling, you got to stop staying in these tawdry places. What are you going to do when Momo isn't around to get you out?"

"I didn't choose it. It chose me."

"Well, let's *vamoose* before they change their minds."

"Drop me in town." Ed said.

"You're not coming back with me to Vallarta?"

"There's something I have to do first. It may take a few weeks."

"Well, Frankie's certainly going to be disappointed."

"Right." said Ed, rather grimly.

Ed gave Emmet an overview of what he was doing but omitted salient details. They promised to meet in Dallas where Emmet was being honored by a theater group that produced his plays only. They called themselves The Stoners. Ed walked the few blocks to the bus station, his bag hoisted on his shoulder. It was midday and Guadalajara's streets were choked with cars, buses, pedestrians, dogs, *burros* and food vendors pushing jangling carts. The cacophony of sounds was pure pleasure after the doom like silence of the prison. No one can appreciate the outside like those that have been on the inside.

CHAPTER 14

Bus to El Paso

His instructions were to travel by bus, preferably *segundo clasa*. He was to take a bus to Aguascaliente and from there another bus to Zacatecas, but with his rudimentary Spanish there was no way for him to find out in Guadalajara when a bus in Aguascaliente left for Zacatecas. Every region of the country had its own bus lines, and one bus line did not provide information for another region's bus line, which meant he might have to spend a night or two in bus stations along the way. From Zacatecas he was supposed to travel up the center of Mexico to Chihuahua and onto Ciudad Juarez.

El Paso was directly across the Rio Grande from Juarez he remembered from his school days. He was to be as incognito as possible for a *guero* among poor Mexicans with chickens and goats and carrying baskets that might be filled with snakes.

The bus that carried him on the first leg of his trip was a converted nineteen twenties school bus with a propensity to rattle. It was painted green and decorated with paintings and objects of superstition. The driver's throne was surrounded by every possible god, saint or good luck diety. Every bus driver in Mexico thought every trip might be his last for often they were forced to navigate hairy mountain passes in dilapidated equipment. More daring drivers like to race each other on lonely empty highways until their buses broke down outside the destination town. Travel weary passengers laden with their bags trudged the few miles to the hotels, town lights beckoning, only to discover every restaurant and cafe closed and the hotels full. "No, I don't have a reservation!" the loud *gringa* would inform the harried desk clerk. "I wasn't planning to spend the night in this dump....which by the way is called what? The desk clerk would say something in Spanish too rapidly for her to understand and other irritable passengers would wrangle with each other. Ed, trying to get comfortable in his hard seat, thought about some of his other trips in Mexico. Looking back, they could be called great adventures, but at the time they were nightmares.

Ed found himself sitting next to the only other *gringo* on the bus, a man wearing a stetson hat, who introduced himself as Hoffman and claimed to be from Milwaukee and enjoying his first trip to Mexico. "What made you decide to travel luxury class?" Ed asked.

"My instructions were to find you, Mr. Martin, and stick to you like glue. I'm your escort and your protector. By the time we reach El Paso you're going to be very glad I'm here. At the very least you'll have someone to talk with." Ed looked around at the sullen, dark skinned *peon* faces, no different than the hundreds of faces that peopled his long history with the country. The bus, upon leaving the traffic snarl of Guadalajara, rolled through the Jalisco hill country, climbing steadily toward the great central plateau. By the time they clattered into Aguascaliente it was already late afternoon, and Ed got off with Hoffman. They found a bus to Zacatecas, but it didn't leave for an hour; so they stretched their legs and Hoffman had a smoke.

"Who do you work for?" Ed wanted to know.

"I wish I knew. I was hired by a friend of a friend I've never met. I'm just one piece of a vast network in which hundreds of people don't know a single person they are in contact with. It's all very mysterious, and the tentacles of this organization run from the U.S. deep into Mexico and up into Canada. I have heard the term Operation Drone Strike. I don't know if that means anything to you, but I have no idea what it is."

Passengers burdened with packages and bundles began boarding, and there it was...the first chicken, squawking and ruffling its feathers. The whole picture came direct from central casting, and Ed almost expected to see a director and his camera crew filming the action. They left Aguascalientes on whatever schedule the driver had somewhere in his head, but some buses in Mexico were considered on time if they arrived the same day as they were expected. The discomfort of traveling no class was weighing on Ed, and he said to Hoffman "This incognito business sucks."

"They know what they're doing," Hoffman replied.

"You don't think I look conspicuous in this crowd?"

"They're probably already searching luxury buses, not to mention airplanes and trains."

"Who is they?"

"People who prefer you never get to El Paso." Ed didn't like the sound of that but he said nothing. Body guard or whatever he was, Ed was not sure he could trust this Hoffman.

The bus shook, rattled and rolled through the desert's star spangled night. He dozed off for awhile until Hoffman poked his arm. "That's Zacatecas up ahead. We need to get another bus for Torreon."

"Doesn't this bus go there?"

"I don't like the look of those two boys behind us. The ones dressed in white"

"Everyone on the bus is dressed in white."

"The ones with the head bands. It looks like a disguise to me. Let's get out to smoke, and, when the bus leaves, just not get back on."

"What about our bags?"

"Forget them. We'll buy new stuff. I may seem paranoid, but I've been doing this stuff for years. I've learned to trust my hunches." Ed decided that with Hoffman this errand for Fowler seemed less risky, although he had not been told there was any danger. Fowler had omitted that little detail.

Zacatecas appeared to be in the middle of nowhere, situated in the high desert, *ranchero* country, as evidenced by the music wailing from the driver's radio. It was three in the morning, and the town, although fairly large, appeared to be completely shut down. Even the porters who worked for tips were sleeping when the bus rolled in. Ed need to use the *bano*. Hoffman went into the station to buy cigarettes. Ed opened the door to one of the two stalls, the vacant one, and saw the largest turd he had ever seen. It filled the toilet, and he knew it wouldn't flush down. He would have to hold it until Chihuahua.

When he got back to the boarding platform the bus had left, but Hoffman was waiting. "Our boys didn't get off. We're safe for now. That's the good news. The bad news is we have to wait eight hours for the next bus." They opted not to get a hotel room and tried dozing on the hard station benches without success. Ed nodded toward an older man in *campesino* garb snoring away, sleeping soundly on the solid wood.

"Look at that guy" he said. "Nothing bothers him."

"Nothing would bother you either if you had a pint of *pulque* in you."

"I've heard that stuff is nasty."

"It's the Mexican equivalent of Clorox."

Ed almost drifted off when Hoffman shook him awake. "There's a fleabag on the corner. At least a couple of hours sleep is better than this." The room was small and the mattress lumpy, and the toilet was in the shower stall. Ed relieved himself before Hoffman showered and was asleep before Hoffman joined him in the bed. Hoffman was asleep before his head hit the pillow.

The next morning they were on the bus to Torreon, and there were no signs they were being followed. Ed tried to catch up on his sleep, and Hoffman worked a crossword puzzle in the English language newspaper he bought at the bus station. "Can you believe they sold this paper in Zacatecas?" Hoffman said. Ed mumbled an incoherent reply. "It's the News. You can get it all over Mexico, wherever there are Americans. But I didn't see any gringos in Zacatecas, let alone Americans. I saw lots of Indians though. We should come back here when we're not on a job. Be tourists." Hoffman muttered to his drowsy seat mate.

What are we? Partners now? Ed thought as he dozed.

"Maybe they were incognito like we are," Ed commented..

"There's no disguise to which I am not wise." He chuckled at his little rhyme and poked Ed in the ribs. "Get it? Wise disguise. I guess I'm a poet…"

"And didn't know it," growled Ed, finishing the cliché. "Now will you leave me the fuck alone, so I can get a wink of sleep?"

"Somebody woke up on the wrong side of the bed." Hoffman chided.

"What bed?" Ed tried to curl up in his seat but ended up resting his head on Hoffman's shoulder.

Hoffman didn't mind. He had been working hard to get Ed to trust him, because it was his experience that people were more easily protected when they trusted you. They didn't question every measure you suggested. They simply did it. *If I say go stand in a corner I want you to go stand in a corner.* In his mind Hoffman shuffled through an entire rogues' gallery of clients whom he had been paid to protect. The ones he liked best were the amenable ones. He didn't need to explain the kind of danger they were in. "Otherwise I wouldn't be here." He liked not having to say that.

He continued to talk to Ed, not bothering to check to see if he was awake. "Nothing gets past me. When it comes to disguise Americans are retarded. Anybody can do it better except maybe Canadians. They might come up with a good look, but the minute they open their mouths it's all over. I met one dressed as a Zapotec shaman, but even speaking in Spanish she said "eh" every other word."

Ed dozed and listened to the rhythmic slapping of the bus tires on the asphalt. Fumes wafted through the inside of the bus, and Ed was forced to sit up and open a window. The fresh air brought him all the way back, and he gave up on sleeping. Hoffman had fallen asleep on his puzzle and was snoring softly. They were passing through a mountainous area, and the views were spectacular.

Verdant valleys flashed past between rocky outcroppings as the bus chugged through tortuous bends and terrifying switchbacks. *I should have stayed sleep* Ed thought.

By midday they were roasting in the desert heat. There was no air conditioning, and the only air coming in through the open windows was oven hot. The bus had become crowded with farmers carrying produce and animals to the large market in Chihuahua. They traveled half a day to get to the market and half the night getting home and would bring back only a few pesos for their time and effort. These farmers were less colorful than their brothers in Chiapas and Guatemala. It occurred to Ed that they were probably poorer and had a harder life, the geography of the northern desert being such that it took real grit to scratch out a living.

When they pulled into Torreon Ed refused to change buses. "I'll take my chances. I'm used to this one, and I like my fellow passengers." He smiled at the faces that had turned to watch his loud, adamant refusal to leave the bus. He had also been exchanging glances with a teenage boy dressed in peasant white and holding a puppy under his arm. The boy was probably just curious. He had been told all *gringos* were *loco*. But sex starved Ed allowed himself an entire fantasy with this boy. What else was there to do on a hot bus on an endless road? Hoffman, who feared a scene above all, (calling attention to themselves was a recipe for disaster) relented, and they stayed on the bus. Ed continued to smile at some of the passengers who smiled and nodded to him.

The sun set and night enveloped the highway. Now there was nothing to see. The bus stopped in the middle of nowhere, and the boy with the puppy got off. *Oh well, there goes that,* thought Ed. Hoffman had awakened and was smoking a cigar. Ed was tempted to rip it from his mouth and throw it out the window. He thought of asking Hoffman not to smoke, but he didn't want to come off as a prima donna. Besides he had to be just as bored as Ed was. Ed was sleeping when they rolled into Chihuahua, and Hoffman left him to go into the station. He came back and shook Ed awake. "There's a bus leaving in one hour for Juarez. We need to be on it."

Juarez! Ed couldn't believe they were finally almost there. They were the width of the Rio Grande away from the good old U.S. of A. He had never thought he would be glad to be back in his own country. Americans! He wanted to go out and hug every one of them, all 350 million.

But they weren't in Juarez yet. They were still in Chihuahua. Something on the bus had to be fixed, and they didn't leave as scheduled. Mechanics labored under the hood, but they couldn't seem to resolve the problem. Every time they test started the motor it died after about ten seconds. Once it lasted thirty seconds before dying. Then all the passengers that had already boarded had to get off. Then the motor started and the driver took the bus around the block, only he was gone for forty-five minutes. When he pulled up all the passengers got back on, and the driver managed to pull away from the curb and into traffic before the engine died. They brought another bus around, but it's engine was sputtering and backfiring, and the passengers refused to board it. Finally four hours after the scheduled departure the bus rolled out of Chihuahua headed for the border.

CHAPTER 15

El Paso

The bus shuddered to a stop in the Juarez station, and Ed half expected a victory cheer from the passengers, but they filed out silently, the ups and downs of bus travel in Mexico being more or less routine for most of them. Walking through the station Ed fingered the slip of paper in his pocket that contained the scrawled address where he was supposed to pick up the package. Ed recognized as fear that claw that was clutching the pit of his stomach. He hadn't felt it since the time he was clinging to a cliff face on El Capitan in Yosemite. Something told him the bad part was yet to come.

Hoffman was sticking with him, and they decided to have breakfast in El Paso. "If I smell one more tamale I'll puke," he told Ed.

"I want bacon and eggs and oatmeal," said Ed, "and I want to eat it in one of those shiny new coffee shops that look like they've been hosed down with disinfectant."

"That's what every *gringo* wants when he gets back to the States. That and watching American TV." Hoffman replied.

They walked across the Rio Grande on a bridge with hundreds of others and walked into customs which didn't ordinarily bother with the people walking across. But they were escorted to a table, and their bags were opened and meticulously searched by custom agents who gave them looks indicating they thought Ed and Hoffman were up to something. The burly one whose name tag read "Cruisank" said, "Where were you in Mexico?"

"Puerto Vallarta" said Ed. Hoffman said nothing, hoping the agents would assume they were together.

"What were you doing there?"

"Vacation."

"You don't look like the kind of people that usually take the bus." he said, opening another bag. Cruisank found a ceramic pot nestled among Hoffmans's t-shirts and socks. He examined it as if it might be a priceless Aztec treasure.

"Hoffman smirked. "One peso at Monte Alban. I'm taking it to my nephew in Galveston."

Cruisank put his ham fist inside the pot to feel around, and the pot broke into five pieces. "Sorry about that," said the agent with a side long glance at the other agent who was inspecting Ed's bag. They finally finished looking for what wasn't there but were sure was. "Welcome to the United States."

They took a cab into the city, and Hoffman said to drop him at Hotel Texas. "You're not coming with me?" Ed asked, quizzically.

"The whole idea of you picking up the package is they don't know you, and they don't know where it is exactly. But the area is being watched."

"Then it being the package I'm picking up."

"Yep." The taxi stopped in front of the Hotel Texas, and Hoffman opened the door.

"And the people watching want to get hold of this package badly enough to cause bodily harm to the person that has it?"

"Correct," Hoffman said, getting out of the cab.

"Thanks for the heads up. I don't know what I'd do without you."

Hoffman leaned back in the window. "I assumed you would have gathered that by now. Meet me back here after you get the package. We'll have dinner."

The taxi sped off, and Ed extracted the paper from his pocket and read the address to the driver. It took about twenty minutes to get through the commercial sector before they drove into a middle class neighborhood of ranch style bungalows with manicured lawns and prim little gardens. Not the sort of neighborhood where you expected a drug lord to hole up. But nothing had been what Ed expected. A housewife woman, wiping her hands on an apron, answered the door. She invited Ed inside. "Morris has been expecting you."

She led him through the house and out the back door to the garage that had been converted into a workshop. The man, Morris, who appeared to be about the same age as Ed, was working on a drone on a work table.

He looked up as Ed walked in. "You don't look like a courier."

"I think that's the whole point of why I'm here."

"I'm fixing this drone to fly into Mexico to pick up drugs. We're going to fly it across in that section of the border that's too rugged for people; so the border patrol doesn't bother with it." He walked over to a cabinet and opened it with a key on a cord around his neck. "I've got two kids; so I don't take any chances." He handed Ed a package colorfully wrapped, not much bigger than a book.

"If anyone wants to see under the wrapping complain loudly - I paid five bucks extra to have that wrapped for my niece's birthday. That usually stops them. But you're not likely to meet up with anyone that nosy. As I said you don't look like a courier."

A boy of about ten years with a shock of red hair wearing a red and white striped t-shirt came rushing into the room, carrying a small drone. "Hey, Pop! Look a blade broke."

"Rowdy, can't you see I'm with a guest," Morris gently reprimanded.

"I'm sorry, Pop. Excuse me, mister," he said to Ed.

"Leave it, and I'll look at it later," Morris told him.

The boy did what he was told, and Morris walked over to another cabinet and took out a bottle whiskey. "You'll stay for a drink?" asked Morris, taking out two glasses. Ed couldn't help checking out his nicely shaped butt, clothed in tight fitting stretch knit. His bare feet were shoed in brown loafers.

"Just one. I have a dinner date."

Morris smiled. "You work fast."

"It's not what you think?" said Ed, holding his drink but not drinking.

"I wasn't thinking anything, and it's none of my business."

"I'm meeting a business associate," said Ed, laying the matter to rest.

"Nice tan," said Morris. I know you were in Mexico but which beach?

"Ah, the good old Bahia de Banderas. I spent some of my most drunken and delirious nights carousing in that part of Mexico. I trust you had a good time?"

"The best, " said Ed, thinking of John.

"I wish you'd stay. Margaret and I can't seem to meet interesting people in El Paso. Between the racists and the back slappers there's not a lot to choose from. Still my work requires me to be here; so we try to make the best of it. I'm sure you have some interesting stories to tell."

"I wish I could stay, but as I said…" Ed was not sure what to make of the vibe he was getting from Morris. Was he flirting while his wife was only thirty feet away?

"Perhaps we'll meet somewhere down the road. I feel the book on the two of us is not closed." He squeezed Ed's hand, warmly. Ed got back in the taxi that was still waiting and rode back to the Hotel Texas. Ed paid the driver and walked into the hotel that was not classy enough to have a doorman.

It was businessman's hotel with a clean, well-tended lobby and comfortable chairs plus an entrance to Cattleman's Restaurant, a prosperous chain of eateries, popular in the Southwest. Ed walked past the entrance without looking at the posted menu, although he was now quite hungry. The man at the desk had told him Hoffman was in room 417. The elevator had a gate that had to be closed by the operator before it would rise, creaking and groaning, to the next floor, and it seemed to take all afternoon to get to the 4th floor. The hallway on that floor was empty of people, but the vividly patterned carpet was worn in places. At room 417 Ed knocked lightly on the door. "Hoffman, it's me, Ed." There was no response from inside, no movement, no voice on the other side. Ed waited a few moments, then knocked again, still no response. Ed thought maybe he should look for Hoffman in the bar, although there was no reason to assume Hoffman was a drinking man. He hadn't seen him sneaking swigs on the bus, and he had not bought a drink at any of the stops. He knocked again. Then he tried the door and to his surprise found it unlocked. It swung open. Hoffman was sitting in front of an open window, back to the door. He was wearing his familiar stetson. "Didn't you hear me knocking?" Ed asked. Ed thought he might be sleeping. He walked up to him and reached out to touch his shoulder, saying softly. "I'm back." Something made him withdraw his hand, a weird feeling. He walked around to the front of the chair. Hoffman was staring out the window but seeing nothing.

CHAPTER 16

Flight to Houston

A million conflicting thoughts ran helter-skelter through Ed's mind, along with the shock of seeing a dead man. He had never seen one before. He didn't run with the sort of crowds that frequently produced them. The world of gangsters and gun play was as foreign to Ed as Africa would be. He had come of age during the Iraq war, but had managed somehow to defer himself out of the military altogether. Ed couldn't see himself in a uniform marching around with a rifle on his shoulder and storming foreign beaches in a rain of fire and explosions. Rather he fancied himself as a sort of philosopher poet, someone who observes life and comments upon it, not one who actively participates in it. Not that he had really given it any thought. Whatever had come before, whatever he had done or not done, it left him unprepared for this moment.

He stood for a few minutes, transfixed but thinking. Plenty of people had seen him in the lobby. He had specifically asked for Hoffman's room at the front desk. The clerk couldn't identify him by name, but he could describe him. The best thing to do would be to slip out a rear exit, making sure he didn't touch anything in the room. It occurred to him for the first time that he might be in danger. He was careful to make sure there was no one in the hallway as he left the room. Instead of taking the creaking old elevator he found a stairway and hastened down four flights taking the steps two at a time. On the ground floor he found a service hallway that led to a back door, passing only one employee, a waiter who looked at him curiously.

The door opened onto an alley, and he walked quickly to the busy cross street and hailed a taxi. "Airport!" he told the driver. Ten minutes later they were pulling up in front of the terminal. He grabbed his duffel that now contained the package he had picked up and walked briskly to the Continental Airlines counter. There was a flight to Houston in two hours. He was very fortunate the prim attendant told him. There had been a cancellation. "It's always wise to make a reservation in advance," she lectured him in a slightly officious tone.

There was a Cattleman's Restaurant just off the Continental waiting room. He went in, sat down at a table and ordered a steak. He wasn't a big meat eater, but *when in Rome* he thought. It had been one hell of a day, and he was very hungry. *He might even eat two* steaks and his stomach growled in agreement. He thought about Hoffman while he waited for his food. Hoffman had told him there was danger attached to the job, but his corpse was the first sign of it. He looked around at the other customers, eating in the restaurant to be sure no one had followed him. But how would he know? He was in the dark about so many things. What was he supposed to do next? Deliver the package, get paid, and get out. Then, somehow find John. That's what he needed to do, and he would have to stay focused.

CHAPTER 17

Houston

At George W. Bush International Airport Ed deplaned with two hundred and thirty other passengers and drifted with the horde and their carry-ons to the ground transportation level. He hadn't a clue as to how to find John, but the immediate priority was delivering the package and collecting $15,000. Until he could dump the package he was sure he was in danger and everyone around him suddenly looked sinister. There was something about the slovenly man traveling with an eight year old girl that looked suspicious. The young couple perhaps returning from a honeymoon and acting all lovey dovey. Was that an act? The spinsterish woman who crocheted on the plane. She didn't look like a hit man, but since when do hit men look like hit men? In the taxi he fished out the scrap of paper and read the address to the driver. "Oh, that's in Meyerland," the driver told him. "Fifty years ago that was *the* place to live. Everybody wanted to live in Meyerland. Now....not so much."

The houses didn't look run down but some yards looked untended. Maybe the Committee to Maintain Real Estate Values had been disbanded. No one would be receiving a note that said "The Committee has noticed that your rose bushes have not been pruned since March, and your sidewalks have been swept less than twice a week. We on the committee feel it is paramount that everyone in Meyerland does his or her part to maintain the high standards we have always enjoyed in our community." Meyerland was a great deal further from the airport than the hotel in El Paso was. Ed had plenty of time to think of his next move.

What had John told him? Something about a neighborhood near a museum. Which museum? Houston must have ten. This was a huge city with as much sprawl as Los Angeles. Then he remembered John talking about a nearby cafe where you could sit outside and see a lot of hot young gay men walk past. He had to find the gay area of town. His best bet would be to find a gay bar and go from there. If he didn't find John he might find a nice cuddle instead.

They pulled up in front of a large ranch style house with a lush green lawn and pretty azalea gardens. Ed pushed the button by the door and heard chimes. Presently a black man in uniform answered the door. "I'm looking for Mr. Philpott," said Ed.

The man asked him to come in and please wait. Presently an older man with a white beard appeared. Ed handed him the package, and Philpott handed him an envelope. Ed knew it contained the money, but he thought it lacked class to count it in front of Philpott. He stuffed it in his jacket pocket, and said, "Thank you."

"Tell Fowler I appreciate all he's done."

"I doubt if I'll ever see him again. I hope I never see him again. Not that I have anything against Fowler. He's been good to me. Only where he is."

"I don't even want to know," said Philpott, disappearing into his house.

Back inside the waiting cab, Ed said, "Take me to the most popular gay bar in Houston."

"That would be the Brad Pit. It's probably not busy at this time, but after ten even a sardine can't get in."

The taxi took him to a residential area of older wood frame houses. "The bar is at the end of that alley," the driver told him. Ed paid him and walked down the alley, bag on shoulder. He knew he was going to have to find a place to stash it. A small neon sign advertised the bar. He hoped there would be a happy hour crowd, but not too big. He had never mastered conversing in a loud, crowded bar. He stepped inside and let his eyes adjust to the dim lighting. There were a dozen people in the bar, and all heads turned as he entered. He walked up to the bar and ordered a coke. Ed wondered if it was wise to carry so much money on his person, an envelope in a jacket pocket. If he could find John maybe he wouldn't have to go to a hotel. With coke in hand he sidled up to one of the men sitting at the bar and showed him a picture of John on his phone. "Know him?"

The man shrugged. "Looks familiar. Maybe he comes here. Lots of cute ones, some even cuter." Ed had never thought of John as cute, but cute could be just another word for gorgeous.. He walked around the bar, showing the picture to others, but none seemed to recognize him until a tall blond man said "That's John Winters. I don't think he comes here. I mostly see him at the Crow's Nest." No, he couldn't say where he lives. Probably somewhere around here. This is the gay area, you know. We call it *Guyveston*.

It was happy hour at the Crow's Nest, and the bar was crowded. Ed was still shouldering his bag and carrying an envelope bursting with money. It was going to be difficult to talk to anyone let alone find his John. He was shoved into a corner, trying to hold the coke in one hand and keep from getting groped with the other. A surge of newcomers pushed one man up against him, who said "Hello, sailor. Would you like to float my boat?"

"I'm looking for someone," Ed told him.

"Aren't we all, honey." He moved away, and Ed managed to talk to his replacement, practically shouting to be heard over the din.

"Do you know John Winters?"

The man nodded. "I think his name is Winters." Ed showed him the picture on his phone. "Yeah. That's him."

"Do you know where he lives?"

"I was at a party there a couple of weeks ago." The man scribbled the address on the envelope with the money and gave him directions on how to find it. Ed thanked him and left the bar, wandering through the shady streets, reading street names off signs until he found the street written on the envelope. A few minutes later he was standing in front of a small wooden bungalow with red brick columns on either side of a brick porch. The front door was open, and through the screen door Ed could see down a long hallway lights toward the back of the house. He rang the doorbell. A tall man somewhat younger than Ed, wearing short tight cut-offs and a tank top, appeared at the door. He looked Ed over before saying "Yes?"

"Is John home?" Ed asked.

"Who wants to know?"

"I'm Ed."

He beckoned Ed inside and then turned and called "Honey, there's an Ed here to see you." A few moments later John appeared. He wore an apron over his tight white briefs, and a question mark on his face. He was wiping his hands with a dish towel. He reddened when he saw it was Ed. Although confused he was really pleased to see him.

"What the....what are you doing here?" he stammered.

"I wanted to see you." There was an awkward silence before Ed continued. "I had some business in Houston; so I thought I'd look you up."

It was obvious John did not know what to say, but the domesticity of the scene was apparent to Ed. He had shown up out of the blue and was now intruding. Ed had not known what to expect. He had harbored the idea that John led some kind of closeted life in Houston, just waiting for Ed to rescue him. Now that fantasy lay in pieces and his head was spinning. He could hear John introducing him to Cory, the man he lived with, and asking where he was staying. Ed had no idea. He couldn't think of what to do next. Suddenly all that he had been through, the arduous bus trip, the death of Hoffman, the dangerous errand, the schlepping all over the cockamamie continent caught up with him. The last thing he saw before losing consciousness was John's beautiful, concerned face.

When Ed opened his eyes the sun was shining through an open window, and a mocking bird was trilling in a nearby Chinaberry tree. The room was sparsely furnished and unfamiliar. Ed was pretty sure he had never been in this room before. In fact he didn't know where he was. Then he decided it must be where Cory and John lived, as the events of the time before came streaming back to him. Besides the single bed, which he was just now sitting up in, there was a small desk with a lap top computer on it. The walls were bare save for a couple of Eugene Delcroix paintings of places in the New Orleans French Quarter in gilded frames. He got out of bed and studied them for ten minutes. Then he realized someone had undressed him, stripped him naked. He hoped it was John. There was a robe draped over the chair, and he put it on. He wandered out into the hallway which led to the kitchen. There he found John at the stove in familiar short black boxers and a black tank top looking as ravishing as Ed remembered. He wanted to take him in his arms and kiss him passionately, but he didn't know if he should. Nothing was the way he thought it would be.

John turned and saw Ed. "Sleeping Beauty is awake before Prince Charming could kiss him. Coffee?" Ed wasn't quite ready to speak; so he nodded. Ed sat down at the table, and John sweetened the coffee with a lump of sugar and added a splash of milk and handed it to Ed. "Just the way you like it."

"You remembered."

John shrugged. "One of the most important things to learn about another person is how they take their coffee."

"How long was I out?"

"Not quite two days. Cory said if you didn't get up by five we'd have to check to make sure you were still alive."

"Where is Cory?" Ed asked.

"Puttering in the garden. He has garden variety garden anxieties."

He joined Ed at the table, which Ed was admiring. "Marmoleum linoleum. Where did you find it?"

"At a junk shop off Montrose. It was painted some awful color and needed repairs. They were going to throw it out, but Cory gave them ten bucks and stripped it himself, refinishing and repairing for days. It was quite a project." Ed looked around, admiring the retro kitchen with laminated Formica counters, a Wedgewood stove, linoleum tiles on the floor and floral farmhouse curtains.

"Who's the decorator? You or Cory?"

"Cory. I make the bucks; so he can express himself. But look at you. I can't believe you're here."

"It's something of a miracle," Ed said "considering all that's happened in the last year."

"What's up?" said John, studying Ed's face. "I can tell something's going on with you."

"I don't know where to begin."

"Start back at when I last saw you in the Vallarta airport, and fill in the blanks."

"That may take a month."

"Then you'd better get started," John said.

Ed told him about leaving Puerto Vallarta and San Blas, about getting stopped and the bag of marijuana. After that came getting busted and hauled off to prison.

"*Campo Muerte?*" John stopped him and called out the back door. "Hey! Cory! Come in here. You have to hear this." When Cory came inside, wiping Vitagrow off his hands, John brought him up to date, and then Ed told them about life in prison and Fowler and the dangerous errand that was going to pay Emmet back for getting him out of the slammer. "Speaking of Emmet he'd kill for those Delcroix paintings you have in the guest room. Would you consider selling them? I'd like to give those to him. How much would you want for them?"

Cory smiled abashedly. "I couldn't sell those. My folks bought those in New Orleans around 1960. They loved going there and took me many times. They hung in our living room for almost as long as I can remember. Sorry."

"I understand....totally," said Ed.

John had been silent; now he changed the subject. "Your story got me thinking," said John. "Last night I noticed a black newer model car parked across street with two men sitting in it. I didn't think anything of it at the time, but now it's still there." They went to the front room to look at it, and that's when Ed told them about Hoffman. "Do you think we should call the police?" John asked.

"Ed shook his head. "I think they'd be very curious too about the package I was paid $15,000 to deliver."

"Would they have to know about that?" asked John.

"You know how police are. They're never satisfied with what you want to tell them. I think for now let's leave the police out of it." Ed replied.

Ed's aversion to the police was showing, but neither John nor Cory seemed the least bit nervous now that murder had been introduced into the scenario. In fact they both seemed excited to have a little mystery/danger in their lives. "I feel like I'm in the middle of an Agatha Christie novel." said John.

Ed shook his head. "No. Raymond Chandler."

"You're both wrong," said Cory. "It's Nancy Drew, girl."

CHAPTER 18

John and Cory

John and Cory were adamant. Ed was not leaving. If he was in danger he was safer with them, and in fact they wanted to protect him and help "get to the slimy bottom of all this. You never know what kind of low life we'll discover," as Cory put it. Reluctantly Ed agreed. His first impulse was to get the hell out. He didn't like putting either of them at risk. And it was going to be difficult to be around John while he still had these feelings. Cory was a sweet guy. If he knew about Vallarta he didn't let on. From the moment they met he treated Ed like an old friend. The whole situation was fraught with if not peril at least messy complications.

At dinner they started making plans. Cory whipped up a tuna casserole, and John took notes. They both wanted Ed to provide more details about his trip. "What I'm wondering is how that pot got under your fender. You don't even smoke pot." John said.

"I was floored when that cop found it. At first I couldn't imagine how it got there. But thinking about it I have my suspicions. I think it was put there before I ever left Puerto Vallarta."

"By someone you know?" Ed nodded. "Who? Who would do that?" John was dumbfounded.

"Someone you know as well."

The dawn broke. "Frankie?" Ed nodded. "That little fucktard. Why?"

"Because he came on to me and I rejected him." Ed knew that John was remembering an incident that occurred at Emmet and Frankie's house, and he didn't want to remind him. "Frankie is used to getting his way, getting anything he wants. It must have come as shock that somebody said no."

Cory was eager to make a plan. Both he and John were sure if they knew what was in the package it would explain everything. Ed wasn't so sure. All along he thought it was drugs. What else could incur such high courier pay? Ed was relieved he hadn't lost the fee. Cory locked it in a metal file cabinet in the office/guest room. Ed was looking forward to the day when he could place that money in Emmet's hands. Emmet, dear Emmet, the friend who had come forward when he was in jail and got him out, using who knows what life savings. His whole history with Emmet flooded past him, and he feared Frankie would destroy Emmet just like he almost destroyed Ed.

It was Cory who suggested that Ed talk to the recipient of the package. "Philpott? He didn't seem very conversant when I made the delivery. I don't know what I expected. Certainly not dinner and a movie. But at least the usual pleasantries. He could have asked me about the trip. He must have known I was in El Paso. How did I get to Houston? Plane, train or bus? I mean people usually ask about these things, but this guy was showing me the door before I handed him the package."

"We have to start somewhere," said Cory.

John came back in the room. "They're back. I looked out a couple of hours ago, and the car wasn't there. I thought they had left, but now it's back. Probably went for Sonic Burgers."

"Not if they're cops. They would have gone for donuts." said Cory.

"How did cops get this reputation for donuts?" Ed wondered.

"Who knows" said Cory "but they go together like cookies and cream."

"And fish and chips," John chimed in.

"Bacon and eggs," Cory offered.

Ed popped up with "Yin and yang."

"Peanut butter and jelly," came from John.

Then Ed said, "Laurel and Hardy."

And Cory and John said "Who?" together.

Cory and Ed waited until the next morning while John was at work to drive over to Meyerland in Cory's Mini Cooper. Ed was able to pick out the Philpott house from memory. A middle-aged, balding man was watering in the front yard. Ed walked up to him and asked "Is Mr. Philpott at home?"

The man shut off the nozzle of the hose and said, "Who?"

"Philpott."

"I'm sorry. I don't know anyone named Philpott. My name is Carson. My wife, Ida, and I have lived here for twenty-five years. Are you sure you have the right address? A lot of these houses look alike."

"Yes, I'm sure. I brought him a package yesterday. A black man answered the door in a butler uniform. Philpott is and older man and has a white beard."

"I'm sorry. I don't have any servants. And there are no men with beards inside. My wife is very ill or I would let you see for yourself if you don't believe me."

Ed looked at the scrap of paper that had the address scrawled on it which happened to still be in his pocket. It was the same number as the one on the plaque next to the front door. "He's lying," said Ed as he got back in the car.

"This is all very puzzling," said Cory. "Is there some detail we've overlooked?" Ed continued to stare at the house, comparing it to the memory he had of it from the afternoon before. Something was different but he couldn't see it. Then he did see it. The azaleas were gone. Someone had gone to a whole lot of trouble. But why?

"Philpott is in that house. I know it. He may be a prisoner."

"We'll come back after dark and nose around," said Cory.

They waited until late, almost midnight, before returning to Meyerland and the house of Philpott or Carson. They drove down the street with the lights off and parked at the end of the block. Cory told John to stay in the car, but John shook his head and said. "Fuck that. I have the flashlight." It remained off, however, as they walked quietly up the street. Across the street in front of the Philpott house they stayed in the shadows among some large bushes. The house was dark. No lights on anywhere. The entire neighborhood was cloaked in somnolent stillness. Not even the moon was up. Cory signaled forward, and they crept quickly across the street, concealing themselves in bushes on the parkway. They checked the house for signs of movement and found none. Then with Cory leading the way they passed along the side of the house and up the driveway. Behind the house there was another building, most likely a converted garage, now perhaps an office or workshop. Light outlined the covering on the only window. No sounds emitted from the house or the little building. It was an ominous stillness.

They huddled together, watching and listening. Ed could feel the warmth of John's body pressed against him and remembered how it felt when they were naked together. He wondered if John was thinking about the same thing. He knew it was no time to be thinking of such things, but the ghost of their not yet dead romance haunted him.

While they were whispering about what they should do next there was a flash of light from the converted garage followed by a loud explosion that shattered the quiet of the neighborhood. Ed, Cory and John were thrown to the pavement, and John split his lip on the concrete of the driveway. They lay where they had fallen, not ready to move. Cory was the first to speak. "What happened?"

"I think someone set off a bomb," said Ed. What was left of the building was now in flames. John took off his t-shirt and staunched the blood flowing from his lip. Ed sidled up next to him and put his arm around John's waist. "Are you okay?" John nodded, his mouth too full of blood to speak. This did not go unnoticed by Cory. Already they could hear the sound of distant sirens. "We'd better vamoose, amigos," said Ed. "If they find us here they'll think we did it."

As they ran to the car lights were coming on in some of the neighboring homes, and even a few people had come out on their lawns. The sirens were louder as they jumped in the car and sped away.

"A bunch of people saw us drive off," said John, looking out the back window.

"It was too dark. They'll barely be able to describe the car much less identify it," said Cory.

"Not to worry." said Ed. "But that was too close for comfort."

There was a bit about the explosion in the Houston Chronicle the next afternoon. Cory had slipped out to go to the neighborhood pharmacy to buy a copy, and they huddled around the paper as Cory read aloud. "It says three people were seen running away from the scene of the explosion and driving off in a newer model car. They were believed to be men, but no one was able to provide a description. The owner of the house in front, Andrew Carson, said he knew of no reason why anyone would do such a thing. His house sustained some damage, scorched paint and broken windows. There were no bodies found in the wreckage of the destroyed building which was thought to be a meth lab."

"No bodies," said Ed. "The place was booby trapped. We were supposed to be the bodies, but the bomb went off too soon. These guys are playing hard ball. What chance do we, amateurs, have against them? If you guys want out you should get out while the getting's good."

"No way," said John. "This is the most exciting thing that's happened in forever."

Ed had mixed feelings about that remark. On the one hand he was glad that they wanted to stick with him despite the danger involved, but on the other hand their affair in Puerto Vallarta had been relegated to what place in John's history of exciting events? More than ever he felt adrift in a sea of emotions.

"Meth lab?" said John. "Drugs? Is that what this is all about?"

"It would seem. And yet that seems too easy." said Ed. "I suppose I could have been carrying a scarce ingredient, but it wasn't as if I was keeping it from them. There has to be another reason for them following me. Why booby trap that building? Why make it look like a meth lab?"

"You think that's what they did?"

"The article say 'burnt paraphernalia was found'. It would be a useful way to throw us and the police off the scent."

"So what do you think they're after?" said John with real concern in his voice.

"I don't know" said Ed. "Or let me put it this way. I know something I don't know I know. Maybe I saw something. Perhaps somebody said something. And I might not remember it because I thought nothing of it at the time. My mind might have dismissed it automatically thinking it was too insignificant to store in my memory."

Ed believed the mind was a department store or rather a compartment store. So when you did your thought and action memory shopping they're all in the same building but not all mingled together. Habits were just actions that the store agreed to take care of for you. It's a service the store offered; so you don't have to think about it. Some memories the store no longer stocked, because there had been no request for those particular memories for a long period of time, such as your favorite food when you were an infant. Ed had entered his own world which he always did when he smoked pot which recently had been not at all. But, when Cory passed him the joint he took a long drag, forgetting completely that he had been clean for over a year now. *Oh, well. Maybe he could drag John off to a meeting. They could both use one.*

He hadn't been able to get John out of his mind. He had no idea where he stood, and being here with John and Cory was a real mind fuck. Unfortunately, being high didn't help him forget John; it made him crave him more. Being in the same room no more than five or ten feet apart for hours at a time, where John was radiating Johnness, left Ed frustrated and edgy.

It was evening, and Ed said he was going for a walk. He pulled on a t-shirt and brushed his lank blond hair back with his hand in front of the hall mirror. "Be careful," said Cory, not looking up from the article he was reading in *Vegetables and You*.

"They're gone," said Ed. "I checked earlier." He opened the door and stepped out into the humid Houston evening, the fragrance of cape jasmine floating on a capricious breeze that wafted in for a few brief seconds before going its fickle way. A radio in a house a few doors down was broadcasting baseball. The Astros were playing somebody. Ed didn't follow sports; he followed art and music and politics to some degree. He could name the nine justices of the Supreme Court, and he knew who was Speaker of the House, and he could name every president back to Herbert Hoover, but if you asked him what bill was passed in the House on Friday he wouldn't have the foggiest idea. In some ways he was beginning to relax. Despite all the potential complications it was good being here with John and Cory. They seemed like family.

He hadn't walked a block when he heard someone coming up behind him. He turned quickly and saw it was John who threw one arm around his neck. "Sorry! You can't be out here alone."

"So you're my protector now?" said Ed as they strolled along together.

"Somebody has to look after you. Look at all the trouble you've gotten into since I last saw you."

"I kind of like the idea of you watching over me. Come to think of it I like everything you do."

They stopped next to a cottonwood tree, and John pressed Ed up against it with his own body, pressing his mouth into Ed's. It was a long kiss. "But I like that best of all," said Ed after taking a big breath. A car rolled past and a teenage boy yelled something from the window.

"So what about Cory? " Ed asked as they continue to walk.

"What about Cory?"

"Aren't you supposed to be his boyfriend?" They came to a small pocket park, a sand box, a jungle gym, one swing, two benches and some grass. They sat on one of the benches. A mosquito buzzed near Ed's ear, and John put his hand on Ed's thigh and squeezed a little.

"Cory picked me up when I was a fucked up kid of eighteen. I was strung out on speed, ecstasy, molly, glue, whatever I could get my hands on. I was practically living on the street or in crack houses. Same difference, full of lowlifes. He took me in, cleaned me up and made me presentable. He'd done very well in his landscaping and interior decorating business and could afford to take time off and pay a lot of attention to me. He gave me a good life. We went to concerts and museums. We traveled;

I became cultured. He paid for my education, and now I'm a junior exec. I owe him everything and he expects nothing."

"He sounds too good to be true."

"He knows I'm not attracted to him, but I give him companionship, and I let him flaunt me. In the gay community there is prestige to be gained and status acquired from the act of parading with a pretty boy on your arm."

"In the gay community shallow runs deep," said Ed. "Doesn't Cory want a boyfriend?"

"Oh, he's had them, but it never lasts."

"You've spoiled him for other men."

John blushed but it was too dark to see. He grabbed a handful of Ed's butt.

"Keep it up. You're turning me on."

"Are you going to come visit me in my room tonight?" Ed asked.

"Maybe."

"Now I won't be able to sleep."

When they got back to the house Cory was all agog. "I hacked into the city's data base and found out that Ernest Philpott, age 75, lives at 2785 Rice Blvd."

"Cory has computer skills," said John.

"A very valuable skill to have, but we're not going there tonight. I've been blown up enough for one week." said Ed. "I think I'll turn in. It's been a long day." He walked down the hall to his room, undressed, brushed his teeth and climbed into bed, covering his naked body with a sheet. He read for a while but the article on growing cauliflower hydroponically was putting him to sleep.

It was deep in the night when Ed awakened to the feel of a warm body against his own. He turned a little and pressed his butt into John's crotch. He felt John's tongue in his ear and his hands caressing his chest and belly and finally his penis which engorged at first touch. After months of lust denied, desire repressed and flat out no action, Ed came to a climax so long and so strong that the guest room curtains would now have to be cleaned. John's mouth sought his and a tongue was thrust deep inside. And, when he was calm again, explosion over, John slipped away. Ed drifted in and out of a dream and then into a dreamless deep sleep, rest coming at last.

CHAPTER 19

Looking for Philpott

In the morning while John was at work, Cory and Ed drove over to West University Place to search for the elusive Philpott. Cory suggested Ed stay out of sight as he would be recognized. "They don't know me from Elvis." Cory boasted. "They'd know you in a nano."

"I won't let you place yourself in danger. Do you agree? Otherwise I'm going to drop it."

"Ew! I love it when you're strict."

A woman holding a vacuum cleaner hose answered the door at 2875 Rice Blvd. The roar of the vacuum cleaner drowned out whatever Cory was saying and likewise her response. "What?" Cory shouted.

The woman held up a suction attachment which she waved in front of Cory while shouting, "Nobody home!" The woman bent over and turned off the machine.

"Would you please take a message?" Cory asked with forced politeness.

"I no secretarium. I house clenser."

"Do you know when they'll be back?"

"I clense house now," she said closing the door.

Cory went back to the car where Ed was waiting. "Nobody there but Helga, the Auswitch cleaning Lady."

"I don't think I want to see her ovens." said Ed.

On Sunday John joined them, and they went back to the Philpott address. There seemed to be no activity. "Maybe there's another address associated with Philpott," John suggested. He began looking on his phone.

Suddenly Ed winced in pain. "What's wrong?" Cory asked

"It's a migraine. I get them occasionally." He shielded his eyes from the sun. "I have some pills I take. Unfortunately they're back at the house."

It was decided that John would stay and watch the house. He would wait in that little pocket park on the corner, while Ed and Cory went back to their house to get the pills.".

"Don't be all day." said John as they got into Cory's car. "I feel sort of naked hanging out here by myself."

"You'll be stopping traffic all afternoon," said Cory.

"That's not funny," Ed heard John say as they drove away.

In the house Ed rummaged through his bag until he found the pills. Ed handed Ed a glass of water and he washed three of them down. Cory with Ed hovering sat down at the computer and googled Ernest Philpott. "What if Ernest Philpott isn't my Philpott?" wondered Ed aloud.

"We'll know momentarily" Cory said

The screen announced 985,000 results. Ernest Philpott living in Houston narrowed it 3,802.

"I hope we can finish by Christmas." said Cory. "Once the parties start you can't get a thing done."

"I think we can eliminate Ernest Philpott who lives in the Heights and who is 37 and works at Outdoorland Sporting Goods. My Philpott is definitely an older man."

"Older men can be cute."

"Well, if you're into white beards" said Ed.

"I always say, a snow man is better than no man." replied Cory.

"Aha!" said Ed. "I think this is our guy. Professor of Nuclear Sciences at Rice University, graduated magna cum laud from Columbia University in 1973. Attended graduate school at Chicago University, awarded a Phd there in 1975. Professor Philpott served as chairman of the President's Nuclear Disarmament Advisory Committee in 1998. He is married with three children and seven grand- children. His wife, Florence Esther Philpott, died in 2004."

"Nuclear disarmament," commented Ed. "We may be over our heads here."

"What was in the package?" Cory asked.

"What package?"

"The package you delivered to Philpott."

"I don't know. I didn't open it. It was about the size of a book and no heavier. Is there a picture of Philpott?"

Cory scrolled down to about midway through the article where there appeared a picture of an older man with a beard. "That's him alright." said Ed. "Now what?"

"There doesn't seem to be any other address associated with him, and, since he's retired, there's no workplace." said Cory "Let's go fetch John. Maybe someone's home now at the Philpott residence."

CHAPTER 20

John Goes Missing

They drove through this quiet neighborhood on this sultry, sticky, summer afternoon. "Good thing your car has air conditioning," commented Ed.

Cory turned up the cold air full blast. "It's against the law in Houston to sell a car without it."

"Is that true?"

"No. But it ought to be. You get used to Houston summers eventually."

"I don't know." Ed shook his head. "Even in Mexico it doesn't get like this except for that hell hole, San Blas."

"I take it San Blas is not one of your favorite places."

"It's hot as Hades. It has more mosquitoes than the entire continent of Africa, and I got arrested there and sent to prison. What's to like?"

"Where's John?" Cory asked as they pulled up in front of the little park where they had left him.

There was no one in the park save for a middle-aged woman with a baby in a carriage which she was gently rocking. She also had a small dog on a leash, a chihuahua/yappy mix which barked at them as they walked up. "Shush, Poppy! You'll wake up Damien." She bent over and gave the dog a light smack on the head. "I just got the little monkey to sleep," she said to Ed and Cory.

"Did you see a young man about our age here in the park about an hour ago?" Cory asked her.

She looked confused, like maybe there was a right and a wrong answer, and, if she picked the wrong answer, it might be a problem. "I don't know," she said.

"A little shorter than my friend, Ed, here. Dark hair, a bit longish, dreamy blue eyes…" Ed gave him a little punch in the side. "He was standing by that tree less than an hour ago."

"I'm not from around here."

Ed stepped in. "He's about yay high," he said, holding his hand up to just under the top of his head. "He was wearing shorts and a green t-shirt."

"He has very nice legs," said Cory. Ed punched him. "Well, he does."

"People come; people go," wafted the woman, rocking a little.

"Did you see anyone answering to that description?" said Cory, his voice rising a couple of octaves.

The woman rose. "I best be getting back. The Colliers don't like it when we stay out too long."

"Where did he go?" Cory asked Ed, who put his arm around Cory's shoulder but didn't answer.

The woman had started pushing the pram but stopped and turned around. "Come to think of it I did see a man get in a car and drive off."

"What did the man look like who got in a car." Cory asked.

"I can't rightly say. We was just walking up when I saw him from maybe a half block away."

Cory had turned away and was biting on his fist. "I got a good look at the car."

"What kind of car was it?" Ed asked.

"A big black one."

"Could you give us some more details?" Cory prodded.

"I'm not a car person, but I could tell it was a nice one."

"Thank you" Ed said to the woman.

"You've been an enormous help," said Cory, his words dripping with sarcasm.

She began pushing the carriage slowly down the sidewalk, leaning in to coo coo at the baby. When she was out of earshot said, "This is not like John. If he was going to leave he would have called me. We always let each other know where we are. He has his phone with him."

"Maybe not anymore." Ed pointed to a smashed cell phone on the ground next to a rock. The glass was shattered. Cory picked it up and examined it. "That his?" Ed asked.

Cory looked closer. "It's hard to tell; it's so messed up. But it's a Samsung. John's phone is a Samsung."

"Call his number."

Cory took out his own phone and clicked on John's number. The messed up phone suddenly started ringing and Cory almost dropped it like a hot potato. He tried to answer the phone but the line was dead. "Now I'm worried."

For the first time Ed noticed a note of hysteria in Cory's voice. He took his hand. "Let's go back to the house and see if we can sort this out." Cory's eyes darted about the scene as if John was there but he was somehow not seeing him.

"We have to look for him." He was teetering on the edge of panic. Slowly they drove through the neighborhood of modest bungalows nestled among large shade trees. It was the hottest part of the afternoon, and there was hardly anyone on the street. Waves of heat rose off the glaring sidewalks. An Asian man crouched among the zinnias in one of the flower beds that fronted a rare two story house. He looked up and waved as they rolled past. A little fat boy on a motorized scooter humming around a corner was passed by a granny on a bicycle. Not another person was out and about, and there was no sign of John anywhere. Leaving the dead stillness of the suburban siesta they moved through more trafficked streets and soon found themselves in the older arbor like enclave of The Montrose.

Before they reached their street Cory braked suddenly. He came to a complete stop in the middle of the block. Fortunately no one was behind him. Ed braced himself with his hand against the dashboard. "What is it?" he asked.

Cory didn't answer. When Ed looked over he was frozen, staring straight ahead but lost somewhere in a jungle of possibilities and probabilities. Ed got out of the car, walked around to the driver's side and opened the door. "Move over. I'll drive." Cory obeyed without once looking at Ed, making no pretense to hide his helplessness. His lover, the love of his life, was missing, maybe kidnapped, and might be in grave and imminent danger. He had to help him but how? He felt helpless, like he was falling with nothing to grab onto.

Ed had a stake in this too, but how could he compare his infatuation to Cory's twelve year devotion. John was Cory's soul mate. To lose him was comparable to losing part of his own body. Ed knew immediately that in addition to searching for John he would have to take care of Cory and keep him from falling apart. Ed's intuition told him he was going to need all the help he could get. There were some really bad people that were calling the shots, and Ed needed to keep his wits about him.

Inside the house and two strong drinks later Cory had calmed back into his highly in control self. "I hope you didn't think I was a complete ninny back there."

Ed was standing next to Cory, and he drew him into an embrace. "We're going to find him. Let's get organized." Ed saw there were two things he had to do. One: help find John. Two: keep Cory from falling apart. Ed was the sort of person who always did what needed to be done. He had the gift of being able to rapidly sort his priorities and was able to make decisions quickly. Putting himself in charge he could clearly see was the only way this could happen. "I think it's time to call the police."

"What if they want to know about the package?"

"If it comes up I'll have to tell them what I know. It's a chance I'll have to take, but we need their resources."

Cory was doubtful. "I know the police. They'll accuse you of smuggling. Let's think this through. There must be something we could try. Let's make the police a last resort. We need an ally. Someone on the inside. But who?"

"Philpott," said Ed.

"Philpott?" Cory was incredulous. "Why he's one of them. He took the goods from you. He's just another gangster."

"I don't think so," said Ed. "I met him. I don't know how he fits into all this, but I know he's a standup guy. Genuine. You know what I mean. It's something you can read in another person the moment you meet them. Like the moment I saw you I could tell you had a loving heart." Cory was a little embarrassed by Ed's forthrightness and wasn't ready with his usual quip. "I'm so sorry you and John got dragged into this. I was afraid this would happen, and now it has. I should never have come here."

Now it was time for Cory to hold Ed. "It's not your fault. You can't help what they do."

"I knew they murdered Hoffman, and I led them straight to you."

"Stop it, Ed. I don't want to hear it. Recriminations won't find John. What about this Philpott?"

"Somehow we have to get a message to him."

"How?"

Ed took a blank sheet of paper out of his journal and wrote one word on it. "HOFFMAN" and under it the number to Cory and John's landline. He folded the paper and put it in an envelope. They drove back to the Philpott house, and Ed got out of the car, glancing around to spot anyone watching. When he was sure it was all clear he walked across the street and placed the envelope in the mailbox. Then he walked nonchalantly back to the car, whistling.

"Why did you creep up, but sashay back, trying to attract attention?" Cory asked.

"I realized we want them to see the message; so what was the point of being sneaky."

Back home it was decided that they would take turns waiting by the phone, one of them always there, while the other would be out buying or preparing food. When it was Ed's turn to cook he decided to make his "famous" tortilla soup, deemed famous because boyfriends who had otherwise rejected his cooking found it acceptable. "It's the cheese," Ed concluded. "Everything tastes better with cheese, and so he was inclined to add cheese to everything he made. When he explained this, Cory said, "I'm surprised you're not big as a house."

"I have one of those metabolisms that allow me to eat whatever I want whenever I want."

"I hate you," said Cory, who was sitting next to the phone reading an Earl Stanley Gardner paperback mystery.

More than twenty four hours had passed since John's disappearance, and Cory began digging in the garden. "I've got to get these tulips out of the ground. They were done months ago." Ed looked on thinking Cory needs to stay occupied, but when Cory came back in the house he seemed lost, not knowing what he was supposed to do next. All resolve had drained from his face which Ed regarded as he sat looking at him. It was a nice face, almost handsome, not as pretty as John's or as young but a handsome face nonetheless. Good bones and nice eyes, warm and trusting. He bent forward and kissed Cory on the mouth. Cory flashed a moment of surprise before returning the kiss with equal ardor. "I don't know what made me do that."

"I liked it," said Cory. "I don't care why."

It was a few nights later the telephone finally rang, and a voice at the other end said, "I would have called sooner but I'm being watched."

"Where are you?" Ed asked.

"I'm in my house, but there's almost always someone with me."

"What do they want with you?"

"They think someone will give them something they want to get something I have."

"Was it in the package I brought you?"

"Exactly."

"How can we help?"

"Get me out of here."

"How?"

"Come at night. 4AM. You have to knock the guard out and tie him up. Find me and untie me. Come tonight because I can't handle much more torture. I will break."

That evening they prepared for their little foray. Cory took a Colt 45 out of a shoe box on the top shelf of their bedroom closet. "Why do you have a gun?" Ed asked.

"This neighborhood can be iffy. Older neighborhoods usually are. I've never used it. I not sure how to use it, but John does."

"I was in the army reserve. They taught me all kinds of stuff I thought was useless at the time," said Ed. "Let me carry it." Cory handed the gun to Ed, who took the gun and stuck it in his belt over his butt.

At a quarter to four they left Cory's house and drove over to West U., driving silently through sleeping neighborhoods. There was no moon; so the streets were dark, the only light coming from lamp posts, making empty rings of amber light.

On Philpott's block they drove with lights off and parked by the park. Before advancing they checked all the parked cars for watching occupants. Then walked silently up the street and moved along the side of Philpott's house and came around to the back door. They pried open the door and entered the dark kitchen from which they could see light from a room and heard the sound of a television. They crept up the hallway and looked into the room. A man was dozing on a sofa and on a straight backed chair was Philpott, bound and gagged. Ed stood behind the sofa, gun ready, and Cory began untying Philpott, removing his gag first.

Although they worked quietly the man on the sofa stirred. He sat up, saw Cory and said "What the fuck...." before Ed conked him on the head with the gun.

Philpott wiped his face and beard with the gag and managed a quick smile. "Let's get out of here before the rest of them come back."

"Once inside Cory's car and speeding away Philpott said "I'm very grateful. You got me out just in time. I don't think I could have held out much longer, and I knew as soon as they got what they wanted they were going to kill me. I even overheard them discussing it."

"We need your help," said Ed.

"Do I know you?" Philpott asked.

"We met once. I brought you a package I picked up in El Paso."

"Yes. I remember now. What's your part in all this?"

`"Our friend disappeared. Some men have been watching us. Somehow we think it's all connected." Cory lit a cigarette and offered one to Philpott who declined it.

"What was in the package I brought. We think it's the key. Was it drugs?"

"No. They are letters, letters written by an important politician, letters that could ruin his career, destroy his credibility. I've hidden them safely until I can return them to the man who wrote them."

Cory spoke up. "We're being followed." Ed turned and looked out the back window of the car. He saw a pair of headlights about a half block behind them. Cory sped up, turned at the next corner and did a U turn; so when the following car turned the corner, they passed them going in the opposite direction. They raced through the somnolent streets of Meyerland, but couldn't shake the other car.

While Cory was zigging and zagging through the night quiet neighborhoods of Houston, Ed talked to Philpott. "One thing puzzles me. I think you were in the front house when the back house blew up. We thought you set a trap for us."

"That wasn't me. I'm just as much a victim as you are. These people don't mess around. They're killers."

They left the neighborhood and jumped on the freeway the other car still behind them.

"What were you doing in Carson's house when I showed up with the package?"

"Feeding his cats. They were camping in Big Bend; so I had a key. I thought it was safer to use his address." Philpott told him.

They had traveled about five miles at breakneck speeds when Cory said "Oops!" Ed turned and looked and saw the shadowing car being pulled over by a by a black and white flashing red and blue. That was the break they needed. Cory slowed down and left the freeway. "I don't think it's safe to go home tonight. Let's get a motel and talk about a plan." Presently they pulled into the parking area of the Vantage Motel. "Let's stay here tonight while we figure out what to do next. I'm exhausted. At least were safe for the moment.

They got a cheap suite at the motel, a reasonably clean freeway hostel, completely lacking in any kind of charm. They made a bed for Philpott on the sofa. In the bedroom the motel's neon sign flashed on and off through their plate glass window, and Cory drew the curtains shut. He stripped off his clothes, and then came around and laid down on top of Ed, who was momentarily surprised. He liked how it felt and soon his hands were caressing Cory's smooth back and feeling up his buttocks. "Why don't you take off your clothes?" Cory whispered in his ear.

CHAPTER 21

Cory and Ed

When Ed awoke in the morning the sun was beating on the one window. Cory was gone and in the morning light the room looked shabby and tawdry. Gone was the dim lit adventure and romance of the night before when two men who hardly knew each other explored each others bodies. Ed was wrenched by repressed desires, and Cory was a ready object with which to satisfy those desires. He found his underwear in the tangle of clothing on the carpeted floor. He was about to pull them on when the door opened and Cory came in carrying a small tray and two steaming cups. "You are a vision to behold. Don't get dressed. I brought hot brown liquid. It's vile but better than no hot coffee at all."

"Barely" said Ed, taking a sip from the cup that Cory handed him. Cory took Ed's penis in the hand that had held the coffee. "Mmmm. Warm," said Ed, starting to get hard. The other hand dropped the boxer briefs it was holding. Then Cory was on his knees, and after taking a gulp of coffee took Ed's penis in his mouth. It took only a few moments for Ed to orgasm. "I could grow to like this" said Ed as Cory wiped his mouth on Ed's t-shirt.

"I assure you the pleasure was all mine," Cory replied.

"Philpott still asleep?" Ed asked.

"He was just stirring when I passed through the front room. I brought him a cup of hot slop too."

"This has all been great fun, but I feel we have to face reality. We're in hiding from dangerous criminals, and we have to find John. We need to make plans." His voice trailed off as he looked down on Cory who was still on his knees, and he felt the strong affection for him. He reached down and pulled him up and kissed him for several minutes, "but I don't want you to think I'm running from you. I like whatever this is we're having, but I want us to take a rain check and save it for the future. Can we do that?" Cory shrugged.

"Let's do what we have to do. I want my John back."

Ed didn't wince, but he was cut nevertheless. It was a rough sea, and it was like trying to navigate a boat without a rudder, having no semblance of control over his situation. Cory wrote on the pad provided by the motel. "We'll need supplies. At some point we'll have to stop by the house."

"Agreed," said Ed. "How much money do we have."

"I can lay my hands on about two thousand. That won't last long, but we can get out of town. My cousin has a cabin in the hill country not far from Austin. He hardly ever uses it. We can hole up there until things blow over here. It's on a lake. It's really pretty up there."

"It sounds more like a honeymoon than a hideout," Ed remarked.

Cory held a pillow in front of his face. "I don't want you to see me blushing."

Ed sat down on the bed beside Cory and took the pad where he had scribbled from his hand and said, "Come here, You." They kissed for a few minutes; then Cory pushed him away.

"We're never going to get anything done while we're together. Go outside for a minute while I work on my list." Ed smiled, pulled on his shorts and went outside. A few minutes later Cory came outside, and they reviewed the list together, while feeling each other up.

"Let's go back inside," said Ed. "I haven't had parking lot sex since I was a teenager."

They drove back to Cory's house, circling the block three times to make sure they weren't being watched or followed, before they parked. They walked briskly into the house, and Cory started throwing items into a couple of back packs. He also grabbed a box from the pantry and began filling it with cans, packages of pasta, boxes of jello, paper plates, utensils, pots and pans. "We won't know until we're up there what we forgot." Cory said. He slapped his face with both hands. "OMG! I almost forgot coffee." He snatched a container from the refrigerator, kissing it before he put it in the box. "The only thing worse than motel coffee is service station coffee. God forbid it comes to that."

They made three trips to the car before they were ready to go. Cory double checked the house to make sure the right lights were on and all the others off. He checked the stove and last of all set the alarm. Then he got behind the wheel of the car and backed out of the driveway before he suddenly threw on the brakes almost throwing Ed against the windshield. "What did we forget?" Ed asked.

"John," Cory said.

CHAPTER 22

John Redux

Cory pulled into a parking place and turned to Ed. "We can't just go off and forget he's in trouble. We have to stay here and find him."

"Do you always wait until you're behind the wheel to freak out?" asked Ed.

"I'm a drama queen," said Cory. "So shoot me."

"It's cool" said Ed "but remind me to wear a helmet in the car."

Cory grinned. "I'm not going to let even one hair on your precious head come to harm. I promise. But I'm a wreck. Maybe you'd better drive." Ed got out and walked around to the driver's side while Cory scooted over.

They stayed parked while Ed began taking charge. "I think our next move is to get Philpott. We have to take him with us. Maybe he can lead us to John, and maybe not. But he's the only shot we got."

They drove back to the motel and picked up Philpott, who was dressed and sitting on the edge of the sofa.

Once back on the busy freeway Cory pushed hard on the accelerator, weaving through the traffic. "Where are we going?" Philpott finally asked.

"Where we'll be safe?" said Ed. "Cory's cousin's cabin. We're going to hide out there and make our plans. We must decide on our next move."

"I really thought they were going to kill me." Philpott said, trembling a little.

"You have something they want; so you're safe until they get it." said Ed. "I on the other hand know something I'm not supposed to know; which makes me a target."

"And what is it that you know?" asked Philpott

"I don't know. If I did I wouldn't tell you. The knowledge could turn you from an asset into a target as well. In the meantime we keep moving."

"Because moving targets are harder to hit" added Cory.

"They have our friend, John," Ed explained. ""He disappeared several days ago, and we're positive it's the same people."

"Have you gone to the police?" Philpott asked.'

"Not yet. Neither one of us have great faith in the police to put it mildly.

But our plan right now is to lay low at the cabin for a few days and come up with some sort of plan. If you have any ideas fill us in. You've actually come face to face with these bastards."

"I was blindfolded most of the time, but I overheard a few things. The way they talked I thought I was a dead man."

"Well, we're glad you're not," said Cory. "And they think they can get away with this shit, but I've got news for them. This isn't over."

By the time they reached the Texas hill country the sun was setting in the west, and the sky was orange with fleecy clouds glittering gold on the treetops in little groves between the mossy green hillocks. A thin mist crept toward them from between the hills, but dissipated before it reached the road. Contented cows chewed their cud, and a lone horse galloped about in a fenced pasture. They passed a field of blue bonnets and another covered with Indian paint brush. At the top of each rise the highway descended at a 60 degree angle and then rose again just as steeply. A great flock of scissor-tailed flycatchers swooped low over the road before tailing off to a thatch of trees among granite outcroppings. Ed dozed with his head on Cory's shoulder and his hand on his thigh, while Philpott slept in the back seat.

They stopped for dinner at Molly's Hog Farm, a diner outside of Bastrop. When they were seated in their booth Philpott excused himself and went to the restroom to "wash up". "I wonder how long he's been holding it," said Ed. "It's been about four hours. He could have gone when we did at the gas station."

"Why didn't he say something. I could have stopped on the road."

"I guess his gratitude for being rescued extended to not being a bother."

"There's such a thing as being too polite," Cory replied.

After dinner they were back on the road, but it was now too dark to see much. They passed through dark forests and moonlit meadows. The turn off the highway led them through a heavily wooded area, and the road branched into a rutted lane shaded by thick sycamores and sturdy oaks. They bumped along this for twenty minutes and finally arrived at a crude log building by a small lake or a large pond which reflected the many trees surrounding it. "The Cabin!" Cory announced.

Ed got out and stretched. "I see why you wanted to come here. It's beautiful."

"My great great grandfather built it a hundred and fifty years ago. He said there was nothing here but a little shack, which some Texans, fleeing from the Alamo, lived in very simply until they all died of the flu one winter." Cory told him.

Cory took the key from under a potted cactus and unlocked the door. They each grabbed a box, bag or two from the car and brought them inside where it was hot and stuffy. They hastened to open windows and let the thick air escape. They closed them again as Cory turned on the room air conditioner. "Let's get all this shit inside" said Cory "and then go for a swim." The inside was furnished simply, one main room with sturdy but comfortable furniture, and a Navajo rug on the floor. There was a small kitchen separated by the main room by a bar. "The bathroom's out there." Cory told them, pointing to the little building through one of the windows. "Try not to use it at night. You might step on a copperhead or a rattler. We've killed a bunch of those suckers."

"I noticed" said Ed, indicating the different snake skins stretched on one wall. "Where do we sleep?" he asked.

Cory pointed to a screened porch behind the main room. "Out there is a bed. Philpott can have the sofa. I hope we have enough propane to keep the a/c on. Otherwise you'll have to do without." he said to Philpott. He went outside and banged his fist on each of the two metal propane tanks. "They're at about 75%. Enough for the time being." He came back inside and said "Let's swim."

They stripped off their clothes, donned flip flops and ran naked to the water, Philpott staying behind to watch and smoke a cigar. "It comes from way up there." Cory pointed through a gap between the trees to a bluish crest in the wavy distance. Ed nodded, not quite grasping the import of Cory's words. "It took some doing to make this livable. Building the cabin was nothing. Laying the pipeline was everything."

They touched penises under water, and Ed started getting engorged. He very much liked Cory's size and the fact that he was uncut. They kissed and swam and kissed some more. The water sparkled in the moonlight. A hawk circled above the trees, swooped and disappeared. After awhile they lay naked on two canvas covered lounges. "I'm liking this a lot" said Ed, softly.

"The cabin?" Cory asked.

"Being with you, Silly. I didn't expect to like it this much."

"I like it too, but we mustn't forget about John. I won't rest until we find him."

"I care too" Ed hastened to add, a little guilty because he might not have been thinking of John's plight for a moment or two.

"What happens with us depends entirely on what happens to John. I can't forget he's in trouble somewhere, and there's nothing we can do." Cory said in ultimatum tones.

"We can go to the police. He's a missing person. I'll risk anything to find him." Ed replied.

Presently Cory left his lounge and joined Ed on his and began caressing Ed's body and soon they melded. They could contain their passion no longer, and words were replaced with physical action. Only moments passed before Ed mounted Cory from behind, fucked him thoroughly and turned him around for the shivering climax, Cory biting and clawing as he shook and shuddered.

They lay in their prospective lounges limp and drained.

"I could grow to like this," Ed said. It was his go to after sex line.

"That's what they all say," Cory replied.

They were in the middle of a candle lit supper when they heard the sound of a car motor approaching on the winding dirt driveway. Philpott visually froze, his fork full of mushroom omelet suspended in midair. They heard the motor turn off and a car door slam. "Who could be coming here at this time of night?" They all had question marks on their faces, but only Cory spoke. There followed a knock on the cabin door, and

Cory got up to answer it. He opened the door, and there in the amber glow of the porch light stood John.

CHAPTER 23

John's Story

After some enthusiastic embracing there followed more embracing. Ed watched tears well up in Cory's eyes as he held John next to him in a smothering hug. He held him for a long time, but when he finally let him go it was Ed's turn. Words would not come. His heavy heart had become so much lighter, but his dilemma was more tangled. From the moment Ed took John in his arms the old desires resurfaced. What now? His first thought was from this point he had to be the passive player to see where the game took him. But maybe the kindest thing to do was to make his exit and let them savor their reunion. Yet he couldn't make himself leave. He was totally drawn to them. He almost could not envision a life without them. Both of them.

John was starving, so Cory gave him the leftovers from the candlelight dinner. "Well, this looks cozy," John commented, giving them one of his sweet John smiles that would disarm an African gorilla and taking a seat at the table.

"We were comforting each other over your absence," said Cory.

"Oh, I see. Is that what they call it now?" John began shoveling food into his mouth, Ed and Cory began bombarding him with questions. "It shasta vait," John said with his mouth full. "I'm eashing."

When they were curled in front of the fireplace, after dinner cognac within reach of Cory and John (Ed still sober), a stack of firewood piled next to the fireplace, a crackling fire to ward off the evening chill, and the three of them touching in some manner, John's head in Cory's lap, Cory's hand in Ed's lap, John holding Ed's hand, they laughed about some remembered time. Philpott had taken up residence on the sofa and snored softly a few feet away. Sweet bluesy music streamed from Cory's phone. "Ok" said Cory. "No more stalling. Tell us what happened."

John began by saying "When you left me in the park I waited by the tree where you last saw me. When the black car we'd seen the night before rolled up, I recognized it immediately, and the two men in the front seat. The one in the passenger seat sort of shouted he had a message from Cory. I walked over to the car, and he said that Cory wanted me to come back to the house because he and Ed needed my help. I was skeptical, but they seemed so familiar with you and Ed I figured you had talked to them. I wasn't sure what was happening; so I thought I'd better call you. I took out my phone and that's when they got out of the car. Your phone hadn't even begun to ring when they took it out of my hands and threw it against the tree. Then they each took one of my arms and dragged me into the car. I was too surprised to put up much of a struggle. They threw me into the back seat and one of them got in beside me. 'We're going for a little drive, John,' he said 'if you don't make a fuss we won't have to knock you out. Sometimes when we knock out people they don't wake up. Just saying....' I was plenty scared by that time. The one in the back with me said his name was Manny, and the driver was Carl.

Soon we were on Westheimer, and when we stopped for a red light I tried to jump out but the door was locked. Manny pulled me by the shirt till his face was in my face. 'Somebody's asking for a knock on the noodle.' Being on Westheimer meant we were heading out of the city, and that made me more nervous than ever."

John sat up a little and Cory hugged him. "Poor baby" he said softly in John' ear. Then he said a little louder, "When I get my hands on them I'll start with decapitation and then move on to torture."

"Don't get your hopes up. These people aren't amateurs. Just ask Philpott."

Philpott emitted a little snort which made them think he might have awakened, but almost immediately his nasal noise became a steady drone with a slight whistle at the end of each exhale.

"They weren't exactly menacing, Manny and Carl; they actually acted friendly, offered me cigarettes and booze. I was too terrified to smoke and drink even if I smoked and drank. Manny said 'Relax. We're just taking you to meet the Chief.' Now I was really scared. These two punks were just the hired help. What could the big cheese want with me."

'I could think of something," said Ed "but I don't think they play on the same team."

"I guess I pictured some sort of hate crime with me being tortured and dismembered. After all this was my first kidnapping."

"It's not the sort of thing you get used to," said Cory.

"We drove into some secluded neighborhood where the houses were further apart, surrounded by trees, mostly pine."

"You must have been near Memorial Park," said Cory.

"We pulled up in front of a nice, big house with a gravel horseshoe driveway under an immense canopy of branches and leaves. A black servant dressed in county squire livery came out and waited by the entrance while my thugs got out and opened my door, escorting me along the flagstone walkway and up the steps to the door held open by the servant. As we passed he said, 'Dr. Gardner is anxious to speak with you. He's been waiting for some time.'

"They ushered me into a small office with a desk and several comfortable chairs. On the walls were large maps of Mexico and the Southwest including Texas. A red marker had been used to draw lines connecting several cities and towns in Mexico to ones in our country. I presumed immediately that they were carrier routes, drugs most likely. A gray haired man wearing glasses sat behind the desk. He looked up as I entered. 'I'm so sorry to take you away from your planned activities for the afternoon, but it was most urgent that I speak to you. I'm going to ask you to do me a favor. I hope there wasn't any unpleasantness.' Well, you can bet I was pissed. 'What about my phone? Your thugs had no business fucking with my phone. It had every one of my contacts. Do you know how long it took me to put my address book on my phone?' He assured me I would be compensated. 'Manny and Carl are good boys, but they sometimes get carried away. You know what I mean?' I didn't and I didn't want to know. 'When can I go home?' I asked him."

Cory got up and walked over to the kitchen area and opened another bottle of cognac. He looked at Ed. "Change your mind?" Ed shook his head no. He filled the two brandy snifters he had brought along from the fireplace and poured golden brown liquid into them. "You don't know what you're missing," he said to Ed. "This stuff goes for seventy-five bucks a fifth at Discount Liquors."

"Just one of the joys of life I'm depriving myself of right now," said Ed.

"If you must self-flagellate I'll show you my collection of whips. It's faster and more fun for everyone else," said Cory.

He returned to the fireplace with the two snifters, handing one to John, who said, "As I was saying about this Gardner guy he wanted me to find out something from Ed. I'm supposed to draw it out in conversation, because it something you don't know you know. And it's about that guy you met in El Paso, Morris, I think."

"I don't know anything about Morris," Ed complained. "I only saw him for a few minutes."

"They know that, but they think you may have seen something that wouldn't register because you wouldn't know its significance. I'm supposed to take notes, write down things you say."

"Surely they would know that you'd tell me this. How would they be able to believe anything you told them?" Ed questioned with open mouth disbelief.

"There was an implied threat, a veiled ultimatum. They gave me a week."

"You were gone four days," Cory said. "What else happened?"

"I told him to fuck off. So he buzzed for Manny and Carl. They showed up and got a little rough. They banged me around a little, but they stayed away from my face."

"If they messed up your face," Cory said. "I'd have to kill them."

"I think they just wanted to scare me; let me know they mean business. The doctor himself was very polite like someone's sweet, old grandfather, wouldn't harm a hair on your head. They were particularly interested in this dude name Morris. They think he's a plant or something. What do they call a spy who works his way into the inner circle of the government? They think the only way they're going to get information from you is from someone with whom you are intimate."

"They know about Puerto Vallarta?" questioned Ed.

"Apparently," answered John.

"Intimate?" said Cory. "That's the first I've heard of it."

"I was going to tell you," said John "but then Ed showed up and..." he sort of threw his hands in the air "the rest his history."

"You've turned me into a character in a cheap Barbara Cartland novel," said Cory. "I hate you."

Philpott, who had awakened in time to hear most of John's story asked, "Did they ever mention me?"

"Just once. They were discussing you in the hallway when Manny and Carl passed my room. I just heard your name, nothing else."

"What would they want with me? I didn't know this Morris fellow. He contacted me once to tell me he had given Ed a package for me and what I was supposed to do with it."

"All this mystery is making me sleepy," announced Cory. "I'm going to bed." He went outside chose one of the chaise lounges and dropped his shorts. He was soon followed by Ed and John who both stripped down to the buff before they climbed on top of Cory. Philpott called out "Good-night!" and switched off the light.

CHAPTER 24

A New Plan is Made

In the morning Cory got up first from his chaise lounge and saw John and Ed sleeping peacefully on theirs. He drove down to the little village that had sprung up where the 310 crossed the 180, where in addition to the gas station and the nail salon there was a little bakery operated by a rather large German couple, Hilda and Klaus. Resisting the proffered strudel he settled for a dozen donuts and bought a Houston Chronicle from the news rack.

Back in the cabin John and Ed were just getting up as Cory returned. John put a kettle on for coffee, and soon they were poring over the story describing the explosion in West University Place. John read aloud in his husky earth voice "Houston police have uncovered evidence in the Carson explosion, evidence proving the cause of the explosion was a bomb. Firing pins and a detonator were found in the carefully sifted ashes. Police spokesperson Haddley Wight said no other information could be provided because it was an ongoing investigation."

That got a snicker from Cory and Ed who said, "They always say that. It's one of their stock lines along with 'So and

So came forward with another witness whose names cannot be released at this time."

"I've noticed" said Cory, "You don't seem to hold our men in blue in very high regard."

"Most of them are morons. That's why."

"Hmm!" said John. "Our situation is more precarious than we think it is. Am I reading you right? On the one hand we have murderous thugs trying to kill us and on the other an incompetent police force to protect us."

"That's exactly what I mean," said Ed.

Ed looked at their faces which looked shocked and word frozen. As if the three of them all at once had come to the exact same conclusion that they were in terrible danger. Then from the sofa Philpott said, "Does it say anything about me?"

Strong coffee and loads of fat and sugar had them ready and buzzing to get back on the case. "I don't really care what they do; I just can't sit around up here as charming and lovely as it is. "Ed was adamant. " We, I mean I have to do something."

"No, you're right the first time. We have to do something. You are not in this alone. And none of us are safe." said John, very firmly.

"Before we involve the police let's try one more thing," said Ed. "Let's talk to this Carson guy one more time. I have this feeling that he's connected, and he knows something."

"Well, it's not much of a plan," commented Cory, "but it's all we got."

They packed and loaded the car, and before pulling out John said "Bye, Cabin. We had a lovely time." They all blew a kiss to the cabin and got in the car. "Does your cabin have a name?" Ed asked.

"Not that I know of, "answered Cory.

"Then I think we should name it Threeway Gardens"

"Perfect," said John.

"I'll bring it up to the cabin committee meeting next month," said Cory.

"What cabin committee?" said John giving Cory a playful punch, something Ed couldn't help noticing. They had this way with each other which only couples who know each other very well can have. He read many things on their faces including the deep caring that could not be hidden.

"Something's missing from your story," said Ed. "You never told us how you knew we were at the cabin" said Ed.

"Cory left me a note. Didn't he tell you?"

"I never gave up hope for one second that you would just reappear as suddenly as you vanished," said Cory. "That's why I wasn't surprised when you showed up."

"I was scared enough for the both of us." John said.

Cory drove with John and Ed up front and Philpott and the bags in the back. Ed liked the warmth of John's leg pressed against his own. He wanted to fondle John, but he felt too awkward with Cory at the wheel. They drove back to Houston in an erotic tissy, their talk avoiding all reference to sex, mostly sharing information about John's abductors and exchanging theories as to what this was all about. The mood in the car was not as somber as the situation demanded. There was excitement to be derived from this adventure. They were enjoying the challenge and even the danger. For a while none of them needed to dwell on their approaching middle age and an assessment of their current positions in life.

Per his request, they dropped Philpott off in Sugarland, where an old friend had agreed to hide him until "this thing blows over," and then drove into the city. They parked a few blocks from the house and took their backyards route in. John wanted to shave. "Although I wasn't uncomfortable, my prison lacked amenities," he told them. Cory made cocktails, and they sank into living room chairs to plan their next moves. "John, do you think you could find Dr. Gardner's house again?" Ed asked.

"I might recognize it if I saw it, but I was blindfolded going in and coming out. I did overhear a few street names I was familiar with like Buffalo Speedway and Kirby Drive. We could drive around in that part of town and see if anything looks familiar."

Cory shot that one down. "And maybe be spotted by Manny and Carl. "Not only do they know where we live; they know our car."

"I think we have to draw them out. Lay a trap," said Ed. "But first let's go see Carson."

The house looked closed, windows shut, drapes pulled, mailbox full, a few newspapers on the porch. Cory banged on the door but there was no response, no sounds issued forth. John pushed the bell a couple of times. A man in the house next door, watching from a front window, came outside and said to them, "If you're looking for Carson, he took his Ida up to some place in New Braunfels. There's a doctor there who says he has the cure for what ails her. I don't think there's anything wrong with her myself, except maybe she's sick in the head."

"Every time I show up they go on vacation," said Cory. "If this keeps up I may take it personally."

Back at the house Ed said, "I've been thinking about a trap we could devise."

"Good. Because I can think of things I'd rather be doing than sitting here in the dark."

"If we do what I have in mind we won't have to. We'll want them to know we're here."

"What do you have in mind?" John asked while massaging Ed's neck. "Boy! You are tight."

"Well, I could say you are too."

From across the room Cory's eyebrows went up. He sat up straight. "Ok. What's the plan?"

"Let them know we have information to share. Arrange a safe place to meet. Then have the police waiting. Pretty simple don't you think."

"Not as simple as our police," said Cory.

"What was I thinking?" said Ed

"We have to try. It's better than just waiting for them to make the next move, wondering what they'll do next." said John. I think it's better if we make the next move, catch them off guard. The best defense is a good offense."

"That's what my high school football coach used to say," Ed said.

"You played football in high school? Somehow I can't picture you as a jock." John let his hand slide down inside Ed's bathrobe and caressed the hard plate of his chest, "but you have managed to stay in shape."

"I didn't play much. Mostly I sat on the bench and prayed Coach wouldn't send me in."

"Don't play modest. I bet you were a regular chick magnet," John teased.

"I had my fun."

"I bet you did. I bet you had a lot of fun." John said suggestively.

Cory got up and went into the water closet next to the pantry. "How much does Cory know about what happened in Puerto Vallarta?" Ed asked

"Not much. When I got back I told him I met somebody I had a good time with while I was there. He didn't press me for details.. I don't think he wanted to know more. We have a totally open relationship, but I know he lives in fear of losing me."

Cory poked his head in the kitchen. "Manny and Carl are back."

They peered between the drapes which were now kept closed day and night. The car was parked directly across the street, and Manny was outside the car, leaning against the driver's door, smoking and passing the cigarette to Carl sitting in the driver's seat. "I wonder how much they get paid," said Cory. "They couldn't look more bored."

"What puzzles me is why they're so interested in Ed," John said.

"I think they think I know something that will reveal their entire operation. It's got to be fear of exposure. What else could it be? They think I saw something when I picked up the package from Morris, unless they think Hoffman told me something before they knocked him off, but I don't think Hoffman knew beans. He was there to protect me, but there was no one to protect him. I think those letters may be a part of it, but only a minor part. If only I knew what I know."

"What about this Morris person?" Cory asked.

"I don't know. I was only there a few minutes. He was very ordinary looking, about my age. He had a wife and a kid; at least I think they were his. He was working on a drone in his workshop and there were lots of parts and tools scattered on his worktable. There were some maps on the wall. Some cabinets and tool boxes. As for his house..."

"Wait a sec," said John. "Did you say something about maps?"

"Yeah. One whole wall was covered with them. I think I remember seeing Mexico and the Southwest and the Caribbean Sea or someplace with lots of water."

"Was there anything on the maps like markings or flags?" John continued to press.

"I remember red push pins were scattered about on the maps, even the major water one."

"Interesting" said Cory, "what the mind sees and stores while we're thinking about something else."

"I think Dr. Gardner knew that. What you're remembering now may be what he wants to know," John said.

"About this trap...got any ideas?" Ed asked.

John nodded in the affirmative. "How would you like to see the Astrodome?"

CHAPTER 25

The Astrodome

At two in the afternoon John placed an envelope in the metal Quonset shaped mail box mounted on a post between the driveway and the front walk of his and Cory's house. The giant sycamore trees were already shedding their hand sized, red, gold and brown leaves, soon to cover the lawn and become an avalanche, the piles reminiscent of Saharan dunes. When he got back in the Mini John said, "The leaves are out of control. When are you going to call that cute lawn boy?"

"You mean Daryll? I believe you scared him off with your incessant drooling." Cory replied.

"I was just being friendly."

"That's what they all say."

"Can I help it if he has an incredibly cute butt? It's the story of my life. Almost everyone I meet has a disappointing butt. Most of them are all caught up in having a big dick, but I could care less. But when I see a cute butt my tongue..."

"That's enough. I get the picture," said Cory as they drove away.

Inside the envelop, hand printed on a single sheet was the following message:

HAVE INFO MEET AT ASTRODOME 2PM TOMORROW

Signed,
The Victims

Manny and Carl were sitting in the black KIA SUV while John put the envelope in the box. Manny got out of the car, crossed the street and took the envelope out of the box. Manny was nonchalant. He whistled as he retrieves the envelope.

Manny and Carl debated as to whether to call Gardner before driving over to the Dome. On Main Street the city dwindled away into solitary restaurants and flat fields. Houston felt like a small town out there. With a few oil derricks and a cow or two and a huge billboard advertising a new development, Briar Bayou, The charm of Louisiana; The convenience of Dallas. The miles of nothing seemed forgotten and neglected, but even overgrown weeds seem preferable to uniform rows of brick houses, all cut from one or two patterns. It's hard to believe people actually live there.

Carl had the drive all planned out, Westheimer to Chimney Rock Road to Main, straight shots and not the worst traffic in Houston, which was affectionately called Snarl City. "Call the number and leave a message. Tell him to meet us there. Otherwise he'll want us to pick him up. Tell him we just heard from the Victims." Nonetheless it took forty-five minutes to get to the Dome. They parked in the weed covered parking area and entered the grounds through a hole in the rusting chain link fence.

"People paid to get in this place?" Carl wondered while he looked around. The Astrodome no longer looked its best. Many of the panes of glass that were part of the geodesic dome were broken or missing altogether. Entrance ways were boarded up, but massive holes in the outer walls gave the impression that no one gave a fuck. Inside, the arena was littered with all kinds of crap, newspapers, broken saw horses, plastic utensils, yellowed programs, their slick covers yellowed and curling. A few rats scurried away as footsteps approached. Thumb sized water bugs scattered as newspapers were kicked aside. "I don't like this place," said Carl. "It stinks and it gives me the heeby jeebies."

"You only have two jobs. Drive the car and do what I say. We have our instructions. We wait for the Doctor." Manny quite often found it necessary to remind Carl of who is in charge.

"I don't like it."

"Nobody cares what you like or don't like. So forget about it. Our job is to follow their instructions to the letter. You know the penalty for not carrying them out exactly. Have you forgotten about Boris?" Carl said nothing more. He knew the smartest thing to do was to shut up, but he still didn't like it.

Manny studied his surroundings, looking for places that could serve as cover, alternative exits in case their entrance should be blocked, places to hide. He spotted the row of offices on the second level. These could be useful rooms if the scenario didn't unfold like they expected. He took a cigarette from a pack of Marlboros and shoved the pack at Carl who waved it away. "Relax. We're dealing with dummies. It only took a few days to scare them into making a deal. All you need is to be a good soldier. Did I ever tell you I was a platoon leader during the war?

"Only a thousand times."

Just then a voice boomed out, echoing in the hollow arena. "Attention! This is the police. We have you completely surrounded. You won't be able to see us but we're here. Now lay down your weapons and go back outside where my men are waiting. If you run you will be shot." Carl looked up and saw the silhouette of a uniformed man behind a frosted glass office door. "Boss, I'm taking a powder."

"Stay right there!" ordered Manny but when he looked around Carl was gone.

What Manny couldn't see was the cassette player sitting on a stool in one of the rooms off the arena and the wires leading to a speaker just outside the door. John had a big giggle at the local spy paraphanalia shop. At one point Cory accosted him. "You're having fun with this aren't you?"

"Whatever are you talking about? What's our budget?" John replied.

John came away with an armload of gadgetry, most of which he never had any use for, but he floored the others with his portrayal of the Captain of the S.W.A.T team. He continued booming over the speaker "Dr. Gardner is under arrest and is now in our custody. Lay face down on the floor with your arms behind you." Manny looked unhappily around and then reluctantly lowered himself to the floor on hands and knees, eyeing the garbage strewn about and the variety of bugs crawling around.

Finally with cheek to concrete he spied an enormous spider marching resolutely toward him. He was struggling to get up when Dr. Gardner and Carl walked into the arena.

"What are you doing?" The Doctor asked.

"The cops told me to get on the floor."

"What cops?"

"The ones that told me to get on the floor..."

"There are no cops here. Did somebody spike your cocoa puffs?" Manny got off the floor, brushing himself off.

Just then John's voice boomed out again. "Attention! This is the police. We have you completely surrounded..." Dr. Gardner moved off in the direction from which the sound was coming. The voice continued booming. "You won't be able to see us but we're here..." Gardner finally arrived at the speaker and the recording device to which it was connected. He kicked over the stool and everything went clattering to the floor.

"Idiots. You've been had. Let's get out of here." They hurriedly made their exit.

In the room on the upper level where Ed, Cory and John had been watching Cory said, "Where are the police?"

John shrugged. "Sgt. Gadfrey said they'd be here at two sharp."

"When did you speak with him?" Cory asked.

"This morning. I told Gadfrey the whole story. He said he was taking it all down." That was true. Gadfrey did write it all down. Then he wadded up the paper and made a nice toss into the nearest wastebasket.

"What was that all about?" asked Sgt. Muldoon.

"Some cock and bull story about mastermind criminals at the Astrodome. Do they really think we have nothing else to do?"

By the third time the booming message repeated Ed, Cory and John were ready to scrap the plan. John looked glum as they packed up their equipment. "It could have worked," he muttered.

"Honey, don't beat yourself up. You just didn't think it through," said Cory.

"Your first mistake was thinking the cops were going to help," said Ed

"Sgt. Gadfrey said they'd be glad to come. They didn't have a thing to do all day."

Cory gave John a brotherly hug. "Our John still has a hard time recognizing sarcasm when he hears it."

"I do not," John protested.

As they left Ed looked around and said, "Cool place. Thanks for showing it to me."

CHAPTER 26

A Mystery Package Arrives

It was on Ed's watch that the delivery truck pulled into the driveway, and the uniformed driver hopped out, leaving the motor running. He placed a package on the doorstep and walked quickly back to his truck, got in and quietly closed his door, backing out silently and melting into the morning shadows. Ed looked at his watch. The florescent dial told him it was 5AM. They had been taking turns standing watch in the attic. Ed was stretched out on an old mattress right under the round window under where the eaves met. From there he could see the street, the yard and the tops of smaller trees but not the porch.

He walked downstairs and paused at the door of Cory and John's bedroom and knocked softly, then pushed the door open and looked in. They were awake, and he could see they had been talking. Cory didn't look very happy.

"I thought I'd better tell you," said Ed. "Some kind of panel delivery truck pulled up into your driveway, and someone put a package on your porch. I couldn't make out the company name. I'm not even sure there was one. Looking down from that window it's hard to see anything directly below you and especially to the side. It was too dark to read the license plate, and he drove away so quickly.

Your street is really dark. You need to petition the city for better street lighting.

"Don't remind me," said Cory. "That's all I've done for the last five years. They keep directing me to departments that don't exist. That's one thing you can say for bureaucracy. They've perfected the art of the runaround.

"The person that brought the package was about John's height and dark complected. Not African American dark but possibly Latino dark. His build was slender to fit. He was not fat or noticeably short. For the second he was in the porch light-remember now I'm directly above- he turned to walk down the steps, and I saw a scar on his left cheek and a reddish mustache."

"Was he cute?" John asked. Cory gave him a little slap.

"Were you expecting a package?" Cory asked John.

"I don't think so."

"Think back. You're forever ordering stuff online and then forgetting you ordered it. We've still never made a single thing from that Ugandan cookbook."

"I hope it's not a bomb" John said. The three looked at each other.

"We'd better check it out," Ed said. They put on robes and went down stairs. When they opened the front door they spotted the package immediately. It was rectangular box wrapped in brown paper. Ed poked it with his toe, and John and Cory put their hands over their ears. "What good is that going to do? If it blows up you'll never hear it." The box didn't explode; it just laid there like a big question mark. Ed prodded it some more, but nothing happened.

"Oh, for fucksake!" said Cory, grabbing the package and walking quickly through the house and tossing it onto the grassy backyard. The three sat down on their patio chairs and stared at it.

"We have to open it," said Cory. "It didn't explode when I carried it through the house and threw it onto the lawn. So, if it's a bomb, motion doesn't trigger it."

"Also the delivery guy carried it," Ed added.

John shrugged. "Let's see what's inside." He picked up the box and put it on the patio table. Carefully they removed the brown paper, exposing a Florsheim shoe box. It was tied with a string. Cory cut the string with the kitchen knife he had grabbed as he went through the kitchen with the box. Inside the shoe box was a Hav-A-Tampa cigar box, and inside the cigar box was a smaller box.

"What the fuck?"

"They're playing games now," said Ed. "Did Dr. Gardner strike you as the playful type?"

"Not in the least" John replied. "But they have tried to keep us guessing. Inside the smaller box was a cigarette box, Turkish Specials.

"I smoked these once," said Cory. "My throat's still sore."

John revealed the contents of the box. It was a photograph of a shrunken human head. John dropped the box like it held a live snake. "If they're trying to scare us they're succeeding."

"But why?" Ed wondered aloud. "They have to keep me alive until they find out if I know what they think I know."

"Maybe they want to scare me and John off; so we hang you out to dry."

Cory said.

"That's not going to happen, John said. "If they want to get to Ed they have to go through us."

"Maybe we should show this to Sgt. Gadfrey," said Cory.

"He was a big help at the Astrodome." said Ed sarcastically.

"Who else is there? I just think we're in over our heads. That's all." John said.

John's right," said Cory. There's no one else that's in a position to protect us. We've got to take it to the police."

"Why not take it to the press? They could demand an investigation."

"Have you seen our newspapers?" Cory said. "We call them funny papers."

"But you're taxpayers." Ed said.

"Tax is a dirty word in Texas." said Cory. "Government itself is suspect."

"You mean we're on our own," said Ed.

"Don't look so glum. We have each other."

John looked out the window. "The sun's up. Who wants pancakes?"

CHAPTER 27

The Best Defense

"I'm sick of waiting for their next move," said Cory. "I think we should go on the offense. Take the show to them. Maybe boil them in oil."

John was standing next to him and said "You're big and you're butch, sweetie pie, but you're no match for those brutes. I wouldn't like it if they harmed one hair on your pretty head." Cory was seated at the table, and John leaned over and kissed the top of his thinning hair.

"Well, what's the plan. I hate that we have no plan." Ed still in his bathrobe came yawning into the kitchen.

"Well, look! Here's old Sleepyhead."

Ed yawned again. "These late nights are getting to me."

"You mean no nights," said John. "Between standing watch and crack of dawn deliveries none of us are getting enough sleep."

"I say we make a plan." shrilled Cory. "Doing anything is better than just sitting."

"Let's go to Gadfrey," said John. "He seemed interested in our situation."

"You could tell that over the phone." Ed wondered aloud.

"Yes!" said John, a little offended. "I'm not incompetent."

"Sorry," said Ed. "I didn't mean to imply you were. I'm skeptical about the police. That's where I see incompetence."

"Well, what other options do we have?" said Cory with some finality.

"I wish I was back at the cabin and none of this existed." John said.

"Then go," said Cory. "You and Ed go to the cabin, have fun. Let me deal with this."

"You mean it?" John asked.

"What's the worst that can happen?" asked Cory. He didn't give them a chance to answer. "Go on! Get out of here."

"I don't like leaving you here to face them alone," said John. "You know what they're capable of."

"I've got sharp eyes and my gun. I'm just looking for an excuse to use it."

It felt good to Ed to be on the road, but at the same time he felt guilty. Now he was getting his chance to be alone with John, and poor Cory was left to guard the house and confront possible killers. It didn't help remembering that Cory was lousy with firearms. What help would he be in a confrontational situation or for that matter John, who had left the street kid far behind? His thoughts of Cory were soon replaced by the anticipation for that which was in store. He knew how he felt about John, and he was pretty sure John felt the same. *But where do we go from here?* The question of Cory who was now his friend loomed large. He knew there was much for himself and John to discuss, but at this moment on a winding road through verdant blue bonnet covered hills and sylvan valleys his heart sprang ahead dancing among frothy clouds in heartbreak blue skies.

Ed was happy for the first time in a long time.

"Why?" he asked.

"Why what?" said John.

"Why did Cory send you off to be with me when he suspects what's between us?"

"He knows he can't stop it. He's hoping it's just another fling. I'll soon be over it and then I'll come back to him."

"And will you get over it soon?" Ed asked

John gave him a dark look. They rolled past patchwork farms on multiple hillsides. "I love this part of Texas" John said. "I grew up in a little town not far from here called Navasota. Not much there but a school, a feed store and a swimming pool. There were some big houses with grand lawns in front and vacant fields and farmland behind. We lived in one of those houses with a wrap around porch, a hen house, a pig sty, and a barn. I saw my first chicken having its neck wrung by our big black maid, Gussy. The lawns were covered with Bermuda grass and burrs would stick in our tender bare feet. My dad owned the feed store; so we were among the better off. I remember walking up the dirt road and coming face to face with a long horned bull behind a fence. I remember the fire escape at the school was rusty metal and during fire drills before it got too cold for short pants we had to slide down the winding tube fire escape scratching our tender thighs. And how I loved to chase after the bigger kids going to the swimming pool. I walked barefoot over hot asphalt, frying cement and burr filled yards to get to that pool. Sometime Sadie who was fourteen and had a bicycle let me ride on her handlebars, making me feel very important.

"I love all that stuff about you," said Ed. "I could listen to you talk all day."

"My family moved to Houston when I was thirteen. When my dad died they sold the feed store and we moved in with my Aunt Tilly, Mom's sister. Dad had left me enough in his will to provide me with a good education. I graduated from Rice University with an Engineering Degree. Then something happened. I changed course abruptly. It might have been drugs. I was doing a lot of them. I decided to take a summer off and go to Europe, backpacking with some frat brats. Then there was Amsterdam where I met Stamos. I fell madly in love. Before that I didn't even know I was gay. It surprised me just as much as everyone else I knew. But I couldn't get enough of Stamos and his friend, Mr. H. Of course, Stamos was a rat, and by the time I was completely strung out and addicted he left me high and dry, running off to Hong Kong with his Chinese whore boy. I managed to fuck my way back to Houston and immediately fell into the gutter with a bunch of other druggies. That's where Cory found me. The rest is history you already know."

John slowed for the turn off to the cabin. "Should we stop in Bastrop for supplies? We left in sort of a hurry."

"You decide. Mostly I feel like I'm along for the ride."

"You've got to knock off that shit. It's not how I see things at all." John slowed and pulled up in front of the little woodsy convenience store at the crossroads. "I'll be right back." And he was with a six pack of beer and a sack full of groceries. When they arrived at the cabin it was still light. Ed got out and stretched before grabbing two bags, while John got the key from under the rock and opened the door. "Home sweet home," he said putting the box he was carrying on the table and opening the two windows.

Was he home at last here with John? Ed asked himself. Besides the excitement he felt regarding their anticipated intimacy he wondered if this was the thing he had been missing. Had he been looking for something that might not even exist? John came up behind him and put his arms around Ed, holding him close from behind, biting gently into Ed's neck. Ed broke free, turned around and took John into his arms, kissing him the way he dreamed of for what seemed the longest time. Moments later their clothes were piles on the floor and they made love on the sofa until it was dark outside. John got up and started lighting candles and the kerosene lamp.

"Don't get dressed," Ed said. "I want to look at you naked."

"You know how cold it gets after dark," said John, pulling on sweat pants and a t-shirt. "Build a fire while I get dinner started." After eating they lay in each others arms on the floor in front of the fireplace on a bearskin rung.

"Did you shoot this bear?" Ed asked.

"One of Cory's ancestors probably did. Cory's family dates back to the Alamo. One of his great great great uncles died there. I'm not exactly sure how they were related, but I've heard the story many times"

"I almost can't believe this is really happening. I'm alone with the person I'm totally crazy about in a cabin in the woods. Am I dreaming?"

"If you are then I am too. It's no different for me." said John.

"You don't know," said Ed "how deeply I'm in love with you. I've never felt this way about anyone before."

"However much you think you love me," said John, "I love you more. Someday I'll find a way to prove it to you."

"Someday? That must mean that you think there's a future for us."

"I can't imagine my life without you in it."

"What about Cory? As far as I can tell you're still a couple."

"Maybe what we are now is a triple. I know I won't give up either one of you to be with the other. I know this is uncharted territory, but if we love one another enough we can make it work. I'm pretty sure Cory feels the same way. That's why he sent us away to work this out."

Ed lay awake that night long after John had fallen asleep in his arms. He loved cradling John like this and feeling his bare skin along the length of his own body. What John was proposing was an arrangement that Ed had never before considered, and yet it made sense. He knew he was attracted to Cory, and maybe before long he would be here with him, experiencing the same joys he was having with John. He knew instinctively that in a triplet there would be no place for jealousy and possessiveness. They would all three be bound with the love they felt for each other. Each of them caring for the other two was the glue that would bind them together.

The next morning Ed was still half dreaming as John made breakfast. It all seemed too good to be true, but here John was naked making him breakfast. John was a treat to watch. Flat tight chest and stomach, nice biceps, a perfect butt, muscled legs all wrapped in smooth skin. There was a light tan on his arms. They were in Houston after all, but the sheer whiteness of his inner thighs made Ed crave to bury his face in them. The miracle was that this beautiful man loved him back, loved him with an intensity that was wholly unexpected.

They spent the day lazing on the platform that was about twenty yards out in the lake. If one of those sudden summer storms common in this part of Texas should arise they would have to swim in choppy waters back to the shore. John swam in their lunch comprised of cold chicken, salad and champagne.

"What are we celebrating?" Ed asked.

"Us." John replied.

"You know I don't drink."

"Just this once. And I'll never ask again." He popped the cork, and frothy liquid bubbled from the bottle. He filled their glasses and held his high. "To us!"

Ed clinked his glass against John's. "To us!" This was followed by a long passionate kiss and lunch.

By mid-afternoon dark clouds had gathered in the north and a fresh wind was at first welcome, but, as it began whipping items on the platform and a few drops of rain stinging their sun soaked bodies, they hurriedly packed up all the items in the waterproof backpack and swam back to shore. They were barely in the cabin when the rain began falling in sheets, a thick mist blew in from the canyon and the wind became delirious. They lay on the bed and watched the rain through the window "Never a dull moment with you, wherever we are," said Ed.

"Would you have it any other way?" asked John.

"Never!"

They were having dinner when the call came in from Cory on John's new cell phone. "They're what?" Ed could hear Cory's frantic voice but not make out what he was saying. John turned to Ed and said. "They're going to burn down our house."

"Let's go!" said Ed, jumping up and throwing a couple of things into a backpack.

"We're coming! Call Gadfrey! Don't say fuck Gadfrey. Call him!"

Ed grabbed a spare rib on the way out, licking sauce off his lips as he chewed it. "Wanna bite?" He offered the rib to John.

"I'd rather just lick your lips." John said as he started the mini.

"That was a great dinner we almost had," Ed said as they wound through night blackened hills. Deep shadows had overtaken the road, but a brightness in the east promised an early moonrise. For now they were a pair of headlights piercing the dark, rushing to a showdown with danger.

John was gritting his teeth, clearly worried about Cory. "Those bastards" he kept muttering. Ed wanted him to slow down on the curves, but he kept silent and trusted in John's driving skills and an empty highway. Grayish hills swept past outside the window, a steady blur lacking in any visible features. Ed reached over and put his hand on John's shoulder, and took his left hand off the wheel to squeeze that hand.

Cory came outside to meet them in the driveway as they pulled up. He had calmed down considerably but the strain showed in his eyes and tight lips. John got out and threw his arms around Cory. "It's okay, babe. We're here now."

"What did they say...exactly?" asked Ed, once they were inside and sitting at the kitchen table in what they now called the War Room. John turned on the flame under the kettle and joined them at the table.

"You can listen to it. I saved it."

A woman's voice came out of Cory's cell phone. "Cory, you haven't been very nice, and we're a little disappointed in you. I thought you were going to help us out. All we want to do is talk to your friend, Ed, but instead you sent him away to somewhere we can't find him. Can you blame us for being impatient, when we've given you every opportunity to cooperate with us? If we don't have Ed in twenty-four hours we're going to burn down your house. Tsk. Tsk. Such a nice house too."

John came behind Cory and put his hands on his shoulders, massaging them gently. He spoke softly in his ear. "Don't worry. We're not going to let anything happen to our house or to any of us. Are you ready to go to the police?"

"Please!"

John turned Cory's head to see the fear in his eyes. "I'll make them pay. I don't know how yet, but I will....if it's the last thing I do."

"This is it," said Ed. "This is the proof we need to take to Gadfrey. He'll have to help us now."

The next day they took the tape to Gadfrey and played it for him. After listening he swiveled in his chair and said, "Sounds like an idle threat to me. These guys are amateurs. You've got nothing to worry about."

CHAPTER 28

Burning Down the House

The plan was for Ed and John to appear to be leaving. They drove away and circled back and parked a few blocks away on a street several blocks south. They scrambled through backyards, ducked under clotheslines, kicked aside plastic tricycles, tossed a football, and skipped over the rusted hood of a T-Bird on cement blocks. Inside their own yard they jumped from the roof of the garage to the roof of the sun porch and from there onto the roof of the house, hanging on to the great limb of the huge sycamore tree that provided most of the shade. From there they crawled down into the attic through the round window in front where they tumbled onto the mattress and into each others arms. John rolled on top of Ed and kissed his face five times.

"Let's not forget why we're here." mumbled Ed, while not exactly resisting.

"I call this our love nest," said John.

They held each other close, allowing the dangers of the moment to vanish from their erotic cocoon. Beneath them in the kitchen Cory waited for the phone to ring, He thumbed through the latest edition of Hanging Gardens and waited, but the phone didn't ring. Eventually he got drowsy and laid his head down on the table, dozing off. Several hours passed. Above in the attic John and Ed made love for the third time. Cory awoke with a start to see a man in a hazmat suit, standing beside him holding a propane weed torch.

"You were warned," he said, pulling the release trigger. A hot flame shot out of the thin barrel, igniting the kitchen curtains. Then he disappeared through the heavy smoke filling the kitchen. Cory jumped up, ran to the utility closet, grabbed a bucket and began filling it from the tap in the sink. Meanwhile the fire was spreading to the window frame and the wall next to it. Cory threw the water at the flames and began refilling the bucket. In his haste he slopped water on the floor and in his rush slipped on it, hitting his head on the tile covered counter and falling in a heap on the floor.

Above in the attic John and Ed smelled the smoke. "Where's that smoke coming from?" said Ed, stomping on the attic stairs. It didn't budge.

"It can only be lowered from below," John said.

"That's crazy," Ed said.

"These old houses have a lot of peculiarities. It's half their charm."

They leaned out the round window and pulled themselves onto the roof. John first and Ed following. Then they swung onto the tree and lowered themselves to the ground. John rushed into the house while Ed turned a jet of water from the garden hose on the fire in the kitchen. John came back out dragging Cory, and Ed rushed over to help him. Cory was still unconscious. John gave him mouth to mouth while Ed pumped his chest. After a long minute Cory started coming around. John looked after him, and Ed grabbed the hose and sprayed the the still smoldering kitchen. A distant siren could be heard growing louder.

The fire trucks arrived in time to keep the fire from spreading to the rest of the house, but the kitchen was a charred smoking hole. Reviewing the damage Ed could see that no meals would be prepared in that kitchen and it was to be difficult to barricade the rest of the house from intrusion. In addition the fumes would linger for weeks, making it impossible to sleep there.

They checked into the Vantage Motel, and the night clerk seemed to recognize them. They stood before him with soot smeared faces and dirty, disheveled clothing. "You're the third throuple this week. *The lunatic, the lover and the poet are of imagination all compact.*"

"It's not what you think," said John.

"*Me thinks the lady doth protest too much.*"

"We had a fire at our house," said Cory. "I almost died."

"*It is a tale told by an idiot, full of sound and fury, signifying nothing.*" He handed them their keys, assuming nothing.

"Just what we needed," said Cory, "a Shakespeare quoting desk clerk. "What next? The claims adjuster will be the Mad Hatter from Alice in Wonderland?"

Ed laughed but John didn't. "What's the matter?" he asked.

"I just remembered the insurance forms we'll have to fill out. Now I'm really pissed. I think it's time to take the game to them." They filed into the motel room and closed the door behind them.

CHAPTER 29

Game On

In the morning Cory and Ed drove back over to their still smoking house. A few people, some Cory recognized, stood around looking. Some shook their heads when they saw Cory. He stepped over the yellow police tape, walked around to the back of the house and began poking in the ashes with a stick. Ed was about to make a joke but thought better of it. He could see the tears welling in Cory's eyes. Cory walked over to the mangled stove. "We got the Wedgewood only last month." Cory said. What the fire didn't destroy the fire department did. "I'm glad we left John at the motel. He doesn't need to see this."

Ed walked over and embraced Cory, holding him tightly. "Go ahead," he said softly. "Let it go." After a few minutes Cory shook himself loose, wiped his eyes with his blackened shirt sleeve and beckoned Ed to follow.

"The police?" he asked.

"The police!" Cory said. "Yes, the fucking police."

Still shaken, Cory let Ed drive back to the motel to pick up John. He couldn't help thinking about their loss. All the special moments with John that took place in that house happened in the kitchen. While making him take his first bath in two years in their kitchen sink and seeing John naked for the first time, he could see under all that dirt and grime a beautiful boy. John splashed water like he feared it, and Cory held and protected him from his daily nightmares. Their first kiss happened in the kitchen, sweet and tender and filled with John's gratitude. What was left of their kitchen was a shambles, and that might be what was left of their relationship. He loved John all the more; now that he saw him slipping away.

At Houston Police Headquarters they met with Lt. Gadfrey, a grim, balding man who chain smoked and coughed incessantly. When John first spoke with him before the Astrodome fiasco he hadn't taken him seriously, but their burned up kitchen forced him to listen. "We spoke on the phone," John reminded him. They had devised a new plan which involved the police. Gadfrey was reluctant to let private citizens become involved in police tactics, but they convinced him there was no way the police could get to the criminals without their involvement. It was Ed's plan, and he laid it out for him.

It involved another person whom Manny, Carl and the others had never seen. This person was Buster Conroy, a longtime friend of Cory and John's.

Buster was short and cute and usually wore cowboy shirts and shorts that showed off his nicely shaped legs and *derriere*. Red tennis shoes and straight dirty blond hair that fell over one eye completed the look that attracted older men by the busload. He never went home alone. The one time he did left him shaken for three days and facing the fact that he was almost forty. Buster was a prankster who livened every party with his antics that ranged from coffee table dancing to a semi-strip show in the bedroom that had guests wiping their genitals on the curtains. Guests loved him and hosts hated him.

Cory and John knew they would have no problem coaxing Buster to join in on their plan with his beat up Volkswagen Bug. There was nothing Buster wouldn't do if he had an audience. Their problem was toning him down for the plan. Asking him to go unnoticed was like asking a group of hypochondriacs not to mention illness. So they asked his advise about the plan, telling him only the details that would apply to the part they were thinking of asking Crandall Misch if he would drive his jeep for them. "Not Crandall Misch!" He almost screamed.

"He's a total nerd and can't be trusted not to blab this all over the donut factory. I'll do it."

"Oh, we could never impose on you. You've been such a good friend to John and I over the years. Helped us out of some many tight scrapes. No, I absolutely refuse to let you put yourself in harms...."

"Shut up! If you let anyone else do it I'll hate you forever."

So Buster was now a key player in a scheme that many would consider cockamamie. But this was nothing new. After John had laid out all the details Ed said, "You're enjoying this aren't you?"

John shrugged. "Maybe."

"I'll do it on one condition. I'm bait."

"No way!" both Cory and John said together. "You're the one they want. They snatch you and make off, and we can't pull this off. What then? They have what they want; so now they can just disappear. If they take one of us then they'll have to stick around," said Cory.

"Look!" said John. "I've been there. It wasn't that scary. They'll think I'm bringing them info they told me to get. I'll tell them the mailbox message routine was getting old, and what I have now may be exactly what they're looking for. Then I'll just babble until the cavalry comes."

Cory and Ed were totally against it. Ed spoke up. "I'm not letting either of you take this risk. I'm the one they want and I'm the ones that's going to do it."

At 5PM Ed stood on the corner as traffic rushed past on Buffalo Speedway. Parked half way down the block on Bissonet was Buster in the Bug. Its dilapidation made it stand out among the sleek compacts that were the trend that year. Also there was black smoke belching from the tail pipe. It didn't help that it was missing a muffler. So Cory was forced to offer up his precious Mini which he called Mimi. She was the second love of his life. They drove over to where Buster was waiting and made him take the wheel, while they drove away, shaking and rumbling in the Bug. "I'm never going to see Mimi again," Cory said while driving back to the motel.

"Oh, please, Cory," John said. You're moaning over your car, and you won't even let me see the house."

At ten after five a black Lincoln SUV pulled up in front of Ed, and Manny got out and opened the back door. "Get in." He gave Ed a shove, causing him to tumble into the backseat.

"Remember the deal was no rough stuff." Ed complained.

"I don't make deals," said Manny. "You don't talk to me. You talk to somebody else."

What was more ominous to Ed was the fact that they hadn't bothered to blindfold him. If they didn't care that he knew the location of their hideout it must mean they weren't planning on leaving him alive. The first little alarm bells started jangling in Ed's mind, making him increasingly nervous. He thought how scared John must have been. He needed to be like John, make jokes, disarm the kidnappers, make them like him. It was easier for John. He was so beautiful and unassuming people couldn't help but like him. He could charm the skin off a viper. His mind wandering was a self-protective measure to avoid thinking of the negative consequences of this little gambit. Was he setting a trap or walking into one?

He wondered why they were so interested in Morris Otto's workshop. What could have been there that went unnoticed? If he could remember he could use it as a bargaining chip, but he hadn't really paid any attention because for one thing he had found Morris Otto sort of attractive and might have been picturing him without clothing as he often did when some male had caught his attention. He might have been a little distracted when Morris handed him the package and his instructions.

Looking out through the backseat window Ed could see they were passing through a nice neighborhood with expensive homes, not mansions but pricey nonetheless. Maybe they were letting him watch because he wasn't familiar with the city. He didn't know where the hell he was. That thought reduced his anxiety. As did the knowledge that Cory and John and Lt. Gadfrey and two more police squad cars were several blocks behind, keeping pace with information relayed by Buster in the Mini, remaining an inconspicuous distance behind.

The area was now completely wooded. Most of the houses were hidden by a screen of pine, beech and sycamore. They turned into a drive almost obscured by bushes and wound through a lush park until a large house loomed before them. It was imposing and decidedly Tudor. They pulled up in front of the house, and Manny got out, opened Ed's door and said, "Get out!" Ed got out stiffly and deliberately walked very slowly toward the front door. Manny shoved him, causing Ed to stumble. "Quit fucking around."

Dr. Gardner met them at the front door. "What no servants? I'm crushed."

"We gave them the day off. In your honor."

"Dr. Gardner, I presume." said Ed, holding out his hand to be shaken.

"We meet... at last," said Gardner, taking his hand. He waved Manny and Carl away with one hand while leading Ed into the interior of the house. "If the urgency of this matter caused you to be inconvenienced, you have my sincere apologies. You may have. Information that is vital to our plans. I need for you to tell me everything you remember about Morris Otto's workshop. The answers I need are there somewhere."

"Why don't you ask Morris what you need to know?."

"I'm afraid that's not possible. He's gone over to the other side."

Despite Dr. Gardner's mild manner, the soft hand clasp, the red rimmed blue eyed stare behind rimless round glasses, the slight hesitancy in his speech, Ed could feel a steel hard resolve, one that could easily plunge a hypodermic needle into his neck or slit his throat with that Lucretia Borgia ring he wore on his pink right hand. "I know you may not consciously recall minor details which at the time appeared too insignificant to register. Memory is a funny thing. It decides on its own accord what the conscious mind is to remember. It's making thousands of split second decisions on its own without direction from the conscious mind. Oh, it may send a memo occasionally: *Memory, please make a note of that lovely building or that pretty young girl.* It may be under strict orders not to forget the milk and butter which the conscious mind failed to put on the shopping list.. Or heaven forbid, not to forget the shopping list itself. But most of the time it's left to its own devices. That is why I have asked my colleague, Dr. Edelmen, here to consult with me on this particular case." Dr. Gardner led him down a brightly lit corridor with a slightly antiseptic odor, possibly concealing a more unpleasant smell. Rooms were divided by floor to ceiling filing cabinets, and Ed imagined scores of young nubile assistants scrambling up and down ladders wearing tight scrubs.

As if reading his mind Gardner said "Ah, but unfortunately... we had to cut our helpers...we've, of course, applied for the Lombard Grant.....can you picture me on a ladder...?" They entered his office to find a white haired, clean, well dressed, close shaven man who held out his hand to be grasped.

"Good afternoon, I am Dr. Edelman. We're very grateful that you have decided to offer... I mean cooperate. It will only take a few minutes to put you under."

"Excuse me?"

"Dr. Edelman is one of the top two or three therapists in the entire country that are well versed in the techniques of hypnotherapy." Gardner explained in his lecture voice.

"We like to think of it as exposure of memory too long hidden in the deep recesses of the unconscious mind. What enchanting stories from the past may be revealed. Perhaps messages from our prehistoric past."

"Did you use to have a big white beard?" Ed asked.

Ed noticed a slight flicker in Edelman's blank eye stare as they shook hands. *Philpott? Could it be?* I think somebody gave you the wrong idea, Doctor Whoeveryouare. There's no way I'm going to let you hypnotize me."

Ed might not have been so cocky had he known that Buster missed the driveway that Carl had turned into. The shrubbery was so thick on this part of the winding road that the only thing that told you there was a driveway was a discreet mailbox that looked like it was part of an oak tree. Buster had stayed far enough back that when he came around the curve the black Lincoln had disappeared completely. About a mile later he figured out that there were driveways, but no amount of back tracking was going to tell him which one had the Lincoln. He called John to relay this information.

"I guess we won't need you anymore. Thanks anyway, Buster."

"You mean I'm not going to get to go to the house? You told me all the attendants wore tight scrubs. I'll be there in a few minutes."

There was nothing John could say that would deter Buster and John knew it.

He hung up and told Gadfrey, who gave him a withering glance. "You think all cops are stupid. We've had our eyes on this bunch for months." He barked into his cell. "Henderson, let the other cars know. We're going in."

Ed wondered where the cops were. They should be busting in about now. He was less than thrilled with the idea of being hypnotized. What if there was gunfire? He might have to act quickly. Edelman was talking in his soft, mellifluous voice. "Do you like my watch?" He was holding up a pocket watch on a silver chain, letting it slowly swing. "It was my father's. He was a respected surgeon in Vienna. It was a gift from the hospital where he worked for twenty-five years." Light reflecting off the watch blurred his vision. "Are you feeling drowsy? It's been such a long day, so much tension, so much stress." Ed knew he had to resist somehow. The doctor continued to drone on. "You need to relax, let the strife of the day slip away, like water down a drain. Don't you find this sofa comfortable? Do you like these soft cushions? They're warm and pliant. This would be such a pleasant spot for a nap. Don't resist. Let go." Dr. Edelman's voice faded away, then returned clear and authoritative. "Raise your right arm." Ed raised his arm. "Take off your shoes."

Ed sat up and began unlacing his tennis shoes. When they were completely unlaced he kicked them off. "Excellent!" said the doctor. "Now your pants." He obeyed, unzipping them and letting them drop to his ankles, then stepping out of them. Edelman walked over, picked them up, folding the pants neatly and putting them with the shoes in one of his desk drawers. Gardner locked the drawer, and put the key in his pocket. Ed stood motionless, waiting for the next command.

Dr. Gardner looked puzzled. "Why take his pants?" he asked.

"If our patient should awaken unexpectedly he won't be as likely to run without pants and shoes. At the very least he'll waste time looking for them." He turned back to Ed. "You are back in Morris Otto's workshop. Describe what you see."

"I see Morris," Ed stated in a monotone. "He has dark hair and a nice ass. I might want to fuck him."

Dr. Gardner exchanged a look with Dr. Edelman. "Sometimes the patient in his hypnotic stupor tells us more than we want to know."

Ed continued to describe, "The studio is not big. Maps of Texas and Mexico cover one wall, and some towns are marked with pushpins. Red ones. A red arrow is drawn from El Paso to Aguascalientes and the number 1127 is scrawled across it. On his worktable are parts of a drone he is assembling. There are some tools, various screw drivers, ball peen hammers, a set of wrenches, wire cutters, duct tape, various materials to make the drones less visible. In addition there is a plate containing what is left of his lunch, an apple core and a bread crust. Next to the plate is an empty soda can. There are papers on the table..."

Dr Gardner leaned forward. "This isn't getting..." but Edelman gestured him to sit back and put two fingers to his lips.

"It's kind of messy," Ed continued. "He points me to the water closet where I pee like a horse. Next to the water closet on the wall are several framed photographs. One is of two men shaking hands. I don't recognize them. The other one is of a man with a dark beard. It could be Dr. Philpott when he was maybe forty."

One wall of Gardner's office was a row of monitor screens with surveillance shots of various points of the grounds, entrance gate, walkway between house and studio, the back fence, driveway, a guest room, cluttered with sex toys and a sling hanging from the ceiling. Ed wondered who used that room. On one of the monitors uniformed men appeared from behind thick bushes and advanced upon the house. Gardner noticed it first and said, "Quickly! Repair to the helipad." He said something in his phone. "Randolph is ready to go. Manny and Carl are with him. He gestured to Edleman to hurry.

"Stand up!" Edelman commanded. Ed stood. "Follow us." They rushed through the house and exited out a back door. Ed found himself unable to resist any of Edelman's commands. On the helipad Ed saw the chopper, blades whirring, ready to ascend. *Don't get on the copter.* He told himself. *Whatever you do don't get on the copter.*

A shot from behind boomed. Ed fell to the ground but was not hit. The noise had startled him from his stupor. He saw Gardner and Edelman boarding the aircraft. They looked back and saw Ed on the ground but decided to leave him, escape taking priority. As the helicopter began lifting off the police began firing. When the whirlybird was about fifty feet in the air a shot hit something making a loud pinging noise. The bird started flying erratically. The next shot hit Randolph, the pilot, and the craft veered sharply downward and crashed into the two story, seven car garage where it burst into flames. John and Cory, followed by Buster and Lt. Gadfrey, ran into the yard, where Ed was trying to stand and threw their arms around him. They all watched the garage burning as a dozen police ran toward the copter. "Well, that's fucked up," said Ed. Buster gave him a lascivious smile and pinched his ass.

Later that afternoon Gadfrey stood in front of Captain Ellis Krike of the Houston Police Force. Gadfrey put his gun and his badge on the Captain's desk. "Oh, for crying out loud, Ornette. Take those back."

"I just want to make one point. I'm a detective. I investigate. I am not the leader of a S.W.A.T. team, although this afternoon I found myself in that position."

"Nobody's faulting you, despite the fact there's over $100,000 dollars in damages the city will have to pay for..."

"Dr. Gardner was a criminal. He was on the verge of launching Operation Drone Strike. He had to be stopped."

"....sooner or later. Now go get a statement from that Ed Martin fellow. He looks ready to bust out of here."

Buster, who had given Ed a ride to the station, waited while he reviewed the typed report and signed it. He flirted with the young desk clerk. "I do love a man in a uniform. Yours is so crisp and blue. He ran his finger along the clerk's collar, and then touched his lip. "You're cute."

"I'm straight.'

"So you think." Buster reached for the clerk's cock, but he slapped his hand away. "I'm a baaaaaad boy," Buster said.

John and Cory had gone back to the house to prep for a little celebration in honor of Ed's narrow escape. After a pit stop at the U-Tote-Em for beer, Buster and Ed arrived at Cory's house. The party was already in progress. The guests were mostly Cory and John's friends, mostly male in the thirty-five to fifty-five age bracket. They had spilled out onto the lawn and were chattering away. A guest that Ed thought looked familiar leaned against the sycamore tree and sipped his beer, while loud music issued forth from the two hastily mounted wall speakers. Later Ed saw him dancing with John.

Ed liked their friends, although he wondered why gay men talked about little else other than their sex lives. "He came across so butch, honey, until we got to the bedroom. Then he throws his legs in the air. What were we supposed to do? Bump pussies?" "I found the most adorable little trick at Puppies the other night. I do love the collegiate crowd, don't you?" Cory led a little tour through the house to see the burned out kitchen. The guests gaped at the blackened hole and the mangled, soot covered appliances.

"Oh my gawd!" someone exclaimed. "It looks like one of Cory's world famous kabobs exploded."

They used the French doors in the dining room to access the back yard where John was tending grill. "Burgers anyone?" he said. A joint was passing from hand to hand, but when it got to Ed he waved it away.

"You don't smoke?" Someone asked.

"Nope. That stuff has brought nothing but trouble into my life." He toasted with his martini. "This is my vice. Salud!" holding his frosted glass high. *So much for sobriety* he thought to himself *but what the fuck...*

At one point after the buffet Cory sidled up to him, kissed his cheek and said "Would you mind taking the Mini to the U-Tote-Em and get some more beers. Better get a case the way these guys are drinking." Ed got in the car, fished the keys out from behind the visor and drove off. The sun was setting on a sultry, windless day leaving a cricket chirping dusk behind. The store was about six blocks away in a heavily treed neighborhood of old bungalows and shady walks.

When Ed drove back up with the beer Buster Conroy was stripping in the front yard to the strong beat of the music. He was down to his briefs and was teasing the salivating men sitting on the lawn watching him. Ed thought he was quite fuckable and made a mental note to ask him out.

"Aren't you afraid the neighbors might object?" Ed asked.

"They're the ones sitting in front," Cory replied.

After Buster finished teasing the men with his peek-a-boo palmetto leaf number the guests began drifting away, and Ed went inside the house where he saw John dancing with a man whose face looked familiar. When John saw Ed they stopped dancing, and John said, "Ed, I want you to meet an old friend. "This is Stamos. We met in Amsterdam a lifetime ago. He's here visiting a cousin who lives in Pasadena."

Ed shook his hand and said "You know I think we already met. Only then you called yourself Morris. Morris Otto."

"In my line of work we're sometimes required to use more than one name."

"And just what is your line of work, Mr. Morris Stamos Otto?"

"I'm setting up a network of drones that can be operated from a central city like Dallas or St. Louis."

"Or El Paso?" Ed offered.

"Or El Paso" Morris agreed.

"And what is the purpose of these drones? What exactly will they be doing, these drones, I mean besides flying in drugs from Mexico? What's their real purpose? Admit it the drugs are for show."

"I'm afraid that information is classified."

"Are you in the military?" Ed asked.

"Not yours." Morris answered.

"So," said Ed. "John's old boyfriend suddenly shows up and coincidentally is my connection for a package to be delivered to Professor Philpot, who went into hiding and resurfaced as a Dr. Edelman. What's wrong with this picture?"

"I assure you it is completely coincidental. I had no idea that you knew John." Morris said.

"Except you people seem to know everything. So why didn't you know I knew John?"

It had grown dark outside, and the party was winding down. Buster boogied his exit with five guys trailing. Ed invited Morris inside and sat with him on the sofa. John offered to make more drinks.

"So tell me what you can tell me about these operating centers and their drones." Ed said.

"I'm afraid it's all very hush hush. Even a little knowledge puts your life in danger."

"It sounds like you're mixed up with some pretty ruthless people."

"Yes. That is unfortunate, but ends justify means." Morris explained.

"Many of us believe means are the ends."

"That's because you are idealists. In these times you have to be more pragmatic."

"The Nazi's were extremely pragmatic. They were so pragmatic millions of people died."

"That's almost a century past. Although we are becoming overpopulated again. Maybe something else will come along like a pandemic perhaps. Ah, but why talk of these unpleasant things? Look at our John. Just as lovely as when I knew him in Amsterdam all those years ago. He's hardly changed a bit. If anything he's even more beautiful and no longer the wild and needy boy. I regret very few things, but dumping John is one of them. It's been a pleasure meeting you." Morris held out his hand, but Ed ignored it. He walked over to where John was speaking with several guests and embraced him and gave him a long goodbye kiss. Then he left, leaving John looking a little dazed.

Ed wasn't the only one that noticed Morris. Cory walked over and said to him. "I don't want that guy hanging around John. He's bad news."

"I think you may be right," said Ed.

"Should we go to Gadfrey?" Cory wondered.

"With what kind of evidence?"

After all the guests had gone, Cory walked around the backyard picking up plastic cups, paper plates, bottle, cans and party detritus. Ed cornered John, gathering clothes to take back to the motel. "I got jealous when I saw you dancing with Morris," Ed said. "You looked like you're still into him."

"Don't be silly. It's you and only you. Been that way since I first laid eyes on you."

"I wish I believed you." Ed was still a little shaken by what had just transpired.

"You'd better start. I won't have it any other way." John had become very serious. He reached over and drew Ed's face to his and kissed him tenderly and then passionately. When they came up for air Ed said. "I can't stop thinking about Morris. I have this terrible feeling that something really bad is going to happen. I'm going to follow him. Find up what he's up to."

"He told me he's going to El Paso tomorrow."

"Then that's where I'm going." Ed took out his cell and dialed American Airlines. "I have to go," he said to John and try to get some evidence we can take to Gadfrey or the FBI or someone. I have to go to El Paso. Are you going to let me go?"

"Yes, but I'm coming with you."

CHAPTER 30

El Paso Redux

On the flight to El Paso Ed and John sat next to each other, sometimes holding hands beneath the little shared blanket that covered their legs. "We're like teenagers," Ed whispered in John's ear. "I can't help it if I can't get enough of you. You're like a drug. I get withdrawals the moment we're separated. This may be a fool's mission. We don't even know where Morris is staying in El Paso."

"We'll just have to smoke him out then." John's confidence was reassuring.

"I'm still not sure this was a good idea. You taking more time off from your work. They must be getting fed up."

"No, they love me at Geo Tech. I brought in several projects under budget, plus brought them new clients worth millions in revenue. I could take a year off, and they'd hold the door for me when I got back."

"I'm glad you came," said Ed. "Let's try to have some fun in El Paso."

The flight attendant appeared and told them to bring their seats to the upright position and stow their trays. "We'll be landing shortly at El Paso International. Make sure you have all your personal belongings, and please turn off all electronic devices."

Shortly after, they were on the ground. In the terminal John waited for their bags, and Ed saw to the rental car. "A Corolla!" John said when he saw it.

"Low profile," Ed said. "He doesn't know we're here. Let's not give him any reason to notice."

They drove directly to The Borderline Hotel. John booked them the most expensive suite in the hotel. Ed frowned. "Why the splurge?"

"Because I want to. I can afford it." They registered under false names and John handed the desk clerk some large bills to cover the first week. In their room John bounced on the bed a few times. "They have valets to walk your dogs. Note to Cory: Let's get a dog. Did you know" he said to Ed, "There's a four star restaurant downstairs? I read about it in that boring magazine in the seat pocket.

"I'm hungry. Let's go eat."

Ed restrained him. "It's early. Let's make a plan."

John drew Ed down on the bed beside him. "I'll agree to any plan that includes getting naked."

They kissed for awhile, but Ed was anxious to get started. "I thought we might take out a want ad. It would say only *Operation Drone Strike* and a cell phone number. Morris is duty bound to check it out. It's too bad we don't have someone with us he doesn't know."

"We could send for Buster. He'd be here like a speeding bullet," John remarked.

"He knows Buster. Everybody knows Buster. What we need is a Buster but not the Buster."

"Philpott would be perfect, but I think he blew up in the helicopter."

"If he really was Edelman. The resemblance between him and Dr. Edelman was striking," Ed agreed.

"I feel like we're caught up in some vast game in which all the players have forgotten the rules."

"No more pot for you," Ed said.

The next day they took out ads in the Sentinel and an underground paper called The Wetback. "Now!" said John, stroking an imaginary mustache "we see if zee feeshies zey neeble." They decided to see the sights while they waited. They drove out to Hueca Tanks Historic Site. "Rocks" said John, looking around. "Where are the tanks?" It was a large jumble of rocks of all sizes, and they watched someone called The Human Fly crawl all over those rocks with no equipment except his fingers and toes.

They took in a show at The Plaza Theater near their hotel, an old movie and a floor show of aging drag queens called the Vaguettes that reminded Ed of old Fellini movies. During the days they braved the Texas sun and hiked in Franklin Mountains State Park. They even went to the zoo to see the rare Amur leopard and the endangered Aruba rattlesnake.

The call came about a week after the ad was placed. It came on the disposable cell Ed had purchased for that purpose. The male voice said "Let me speak to Hiram."

It was Ed that answered. "Hiram's not here right now. May I take a message?"

It was silent at the other end for a moment, then the caller spoke again. "Tell Hiram I'm interested in the job. He should call this number, 873 457-6974. The best time to reach me is after 7PM."

"We have a customer," Ed said to John, clicking the phone to off.

"Just in time," John replied. "I think we've seen all El Paso has to offer."

"You keep acting like we're on some kind of holiday," Ed said, grinning.

"We're not?" said John, pulling Ed down beside him on the bed."

"I wish you take this thing seriously. These are dangerous people we're dealing with."

"Honey, saving the world is my number one priority. But in my spare time......!" John sprang up and smothered Ed's body with his own. Ed lay back, surrendering, but he had this strange feeling that they were blundering into something they wouldn't be able to control.

"It's almost seven," Ed said.

"You make the call. They know my voice. Distort yours a little." He handed his handkerchief to Ed, who put it up to his nose and inhaled the scent.

John noticed and smiled. "You perv." Ed dialed the number. "Tell them Gardner sent us."

Ed shook his head. "No. They're bound to have heard of his death. It got a lot of news coverage." He mused for a moment. "I'm thinking of using Hoffman. It's logical they would assume Hoffman would have tried to give me some information before they got to him. I'll let them think he succeeded." A woman answered, and Ed said. "Hoffman gave me this number. He said it anything happened to him I should get in touch with you. I have a package. I should say *had* a package. I mailed it to Morris Otto, general delivery, El Paso Central Post Office.

Two days later they went to the post office and waited outside for someone to appear carrying a package wrapped in green and red Christmas paper with little bells tinkling from the fancy ribbon. When Ed questioned John about the wrapping "It's August. Why the tinsel?"

John responded "How else are we going to recognize the person picking up. It's not likely Stamos will come down to get it in person."

"Why do you call him Stamos? He calls himself Morris Otto."

John gave Ed a look that chilled him. "Stamos is the past. He is now Morris Otto, and we will never mention Stamos again." Ed nodded in agreement, but he was far from satisfied. Whatever John wanted to call him; he loomed large in their present. And he could not shake the feeling that there was a stronger connection between John and Morris than John was willing to admit.

He was lost in these thoughts and didn't notice at first that John was nudging him. A woman was leaving the post office carrying the garishly wrapped package. The bells on the package tinkled as she walked right past them. They walked briskly to the rental car, parked at a nearby meter, and jumped in with John driving, staying a block behind the woman with the package in her red Prius. Something flapped on the rental car windshield, and Ed took the wheel while John stood, leaned forward, snatched it off the windshield wiper and handed it to Ed.

"What is it?" he asked.

"Overtime parking," said Ed.

"Those bastards."

They followed the red car through heavy afternoon traffic which thinned as they moved through the flat suburbs of rectangular boxes with cacti and succulents in their sandy yards. They were thirty miles into the desert where ocotillo bloomed by day and coyotes howled at night. The red car finally turned off the main road into what looked like a dirt driveway leading up to a two story wood frame building with peeling paint and a weed choked yard. They drove past and turned around a mile later and found a place to stash the car a few blocks away. Staying behind a clump of bushes they watched the woman talking with some man as they walked up the path to the porch. "San Miguel is paying for it.

No one cares that Guanajuato loses money. I've got good people there."

The man said "No one questions your choice of employees, Edith. We're just concerned..." His voice tailed off" as they went inside, closing the door behind them. John and Ed crept to the window. They could see the two arguing, but their voice were muffled. At one point the man almost shouted "Guanajuato is hemorrhaging cash. They don't want it to go on."

"Who is they?" Edith asked.

"This came from Morris himself."

"I think this is it," Ed whispered. "Command central. The nexus. The nest."

"What next?" John wanted to know.

"We come back tonight and set it on fire," Ed replied.

They drove back to the hotel, stopping at a hardware store to buy a gas can and at a Texaco station to fill the can with gasoline. They left it in the trunk of the car in the hotel parking lot and went back to their room to shower and shave. They had a meaty dinner at Cattleman's, a restaurant off the lobby of the hotel. "Does every hotel have one of these?" Ed asked.

"There are at least fifteen in El Paso and fifteen more in Austin," John replied.

"What about San Antonio and Houston?"

"The County Line Restaurant keeps San Antonians and their tourists stuffed, while Houston oilmen have their happy hour at Jackson's Watering Hole."

"I heard there was nothing in Texas but steers and queers." Ed said, reaching under the table to grope John.

"I don't hear you complaining." John replied.

At midnight they drove back to the house in the desert. They crept up to the front porch and crammed dry brush and tree limbs under it. John poured gasoline from the can onto the brush. They could hear voices in the house, and lights were on in several rooms. They worked quickly, and as soon as John lit the brush they scampered back into the shadows to watch. The fire smoked a bit before flaring up, but the wood framed porch caught quickly and within a few minutes spread to the upper floor of the house. Then there were voices yelling and someone flew out the front door, leaping over the flaming porch. Two more men came running from the back of the house and joined the other man in the yard. The woman appeared in the upstairs window screaming. "I can't get down. The stairs are on fire."

"Jump!" one of the men yelled.

She hesitated, but with flames licking at her back she had no choice. She crawled out the window and clung to the sill before letting go. She hit the ground with a thud, and one of the men walked over to where she landed. "Are you okay?" they heard him say. They couldn't hear her reply. Her voice was muffled, but they saw the man help her up and help her walk to her car, the red one. Soon fire trucks, sirens blaring, arrived on the scene and began spraying water until the house was a black smoldering shell. In the commotion, the occupants of the house drove away too swiftly for Ed and John to follow.

Later they looked at pictures of the blaze on Ed's phone. "I always wanted to burn a house down." said John. "It was real *purdy*" John said, doing his hillbilly hottie in his tighty whities and dancing around just out of Ed's reach.

"We could have killed those people in the house," Ed said.

"And how many people did we keep them from killing?" John asked.

"We burned them out, but that's not going to stop them. It may delay them, depending upon what else was in the house, plans, notes, maps, equipment, drones. We have to get their leader. Cut off the head and the body runs amok."

"And who is the leader?" John wondered.

"I wish I knew. Maybe Morris."

"Lay off Morris. We haven't even laid eyes on him. He may not have anything to do with any of this." He walked into the bathroom, saying. "I'm going to brush my teeth and crash. I'm out of it." Ed stared at the closed door. Ed hated the way

John got defensive anytime the subject of Morris/Stamos came up. When John came out of the bathroom Ed was already in bed with the light out. John crawled into bed, but instead of snuggling up to Ed he stayed on his side of the bed and was soon asleep. Ed on the other hand was wide awake, staring at the wall.

CHAPTER 31

The Garden Path

When the response came from Operation Drone Strike it was as cryptic as anything that had come before. John and Ed had decided to take in a movie at the Fox Orpheum, an old movie palace in the heart of old El Paso dedicated to showing cinema classics. The feature after a Bugs Bunny cartoon and an old newsreel was Mildred Pierce which Ed insisted John had to see. "You're thirty and you've never seen Mildred Pierce? This should be in Ripley's Believe It or Not."

"I've been busy. Self-educating. I hadn't gotten around to it."

"Next you're going to tell me you don't know who Joan Crawford is." Ed continued looking appalled.

"Everybody knows who Joan Crawford was. She owned Pepsi," John said with a triumphant smirk.

"She's a fucking icon. You may have to surrender your gay card. Next you're going to tell me you don't know who Bette Davis is."

"Of course I know Bette. She's one of the Golden Girls."

Ed looked shocked in disbelief. "I blame Cory. He's neglected this part of your education. How do you even carry on a conversation with his queeny friends?"

John was beginning to look offended. "We manage. I just make them think I might be available, and the rest of it doesn't matter."

"I'm sorry," said Ed. "I guess I've spent too much time around Emmet. You begin to take certain things for granted, one thing being that everyone you know shares the same movie references."

"Does that mean you don't love me anymore....because I don't know movies."

"*Au contraire*. I love you the more because you are this raw, innocent thing blowing in the wind."

"Is that a nice way of telling me I'm ignorant?"

"I love exactly what you are. I wouldn't change one hair on your pretty head." Ed brushed his lips across John's face, seeking his lips, but John turned his head away.

"Is that all I am to you...a pretty face?"

Ed pushed John away from him. "Cut it out! Why are you doing this? Why are you questioning how I feel? You're the one...."

"I'm the one what?"

"I've seen how you are with Morris. Or should I say Stamos." John got off the bed and backed slowly to the door.

"I can't believe you went there. After what I've said. After what I thought we meant to each other. Have I been a fool?" He turned and walked out of the room, slamming the door. Ed's heart was in his stomach and a loud clashing noise filled his head. They never made it to the movie. John returned in a few hours, smelling of alcohol as he flung off his clothes and crawled into bed. Ed didn't tell John there was a message from ODS. He had gone down to the news stand in the lobby to buy aspirin and saw the message in their box behind the desk. The desk clerk didn't know who left it, having just begun his shift twelve minutes before. There was nothing in the envelope but a business card for a restaurant in San Francisco, Louis Gevant on Lombard Street. On the back was written Monday 2PM.

In the morning he showed the card to John, the tensions of the past evening having evaporated, both determined to move on from last night's rare spat. "I've always wanted to go to San Francisco," John said.

Ed made reservations on a flight to San Francisco for the following day. "Are you sorry we're leaving?" Ed asked.

John rolled his eyes. "I think we've wrung the last bit of fun from El Paso. Who would have thought there was even this much to do or see in El Puto?"

"Be nice. It's not every day we get to burn a house."

John went over to Ed and put his arms around him. "How will we ever top that?"

Ed looked into John's eyes. "Are you going to be restless when we're no longer living dangerously?"

John shrugged. "Who knows. I'm no fortune teller. All I can tell you is how I feel right now...." John paused. "I'm mad for you."

"That's good enough for me." Ed said, sliding into their intimacy.

"No, you don't understand. I no longer care about myself. I only care about you. I'm not sure that's healthy."

"Since I feel the same about you, we'll care for each other. That's healthy."

Ed concluded.

With their relationship seemingly settled Ed relaxed a little. They enjoyed the flight, laughing at cartoons in somebody's discarded *New Yorker*. They seemed more like a couple now. Ed didn't have to fear that John could just disappear from his life for a variety of reasons. At last a commitment had been made *or had it?* He chose for the time being to think it had.

CHAPTER 32

San Francisco

"How should I dress?" asked John as he put his socks and underwear in the dresser. "I'll take the top drawer if that's okay."

"Nice," Ed answered. "San Francisco can be a little pissy if you know what I mean."

"I come from the deep South. Those queens sweat too much to get pissy. You'll have to show me."

"Wear a jacket," Ed said.

They left the hotel and decided to stroll through Chinatown before calling an Uber. "There's a bar around here I used to go to." Ed said.

"You lived here?" John asked.

"Right out of college. I thought I was straight then. I came here with my girlfriend, Debbie, and we had an apartment by the Medical Center. She was training to be a nurse. I used to swim at the YMCA and then steam in their large steam room. One day I was in there with two guys, and they started hitting on me. Of course, I liked it, but I wasn't ready to do anything. They didn't give me a choice. One of them held me down while the other one raped me. Afterward I realized I liked it, and started looking for gay guys to have sex with. The rest is history."

"You call your whoredom history." John laughed.

"Let's face it," Ed said. "All men are whores."

"And gay men?"

"Sluts," Ed replied.

In Chinatown they browsed the myriad shops cluttered with gleaming buddhas and red paper lanterns. Incense wafted over Grant Avenue, and a slinky black clad proprietress was waiting in each store to lure them in. John held up a small bell and shook it, glancing at the Chinese woman by the door who remained impassive. A couple of boys set off fire crackers on the sidewalk, and a lanky Asian youth pedaled a bicycle cart up the street carrying a large woven basket. "Here" said Ed, stopping at a glass fronted cafe. "This place used to be really good. We can lunch here and easily get to Louis Gevant by 2PM." The sign said Sydney Choos Foo Yoo Palace. They went in and sat in a polished mahogany booth, upholstered in dark green leatherette. The waiter, a pretty Chinese boy, brought them two large glossy menus.

"Did you see him?" asked John. "He's exquisite, like a porcelain doll."

"I don't know why but Asians never did much for me. Not meaty enough I suppose."

"I never took you for a size queen."

"I'm not," Ed protested. "I've always found a lot of ways to get off."

The waiter brought their lunch and dished out platefuls of noodles and sprouts. John immediately began to struggle with the chop sticks. "Don't tell me you've never used chopsticks before."

"I never got the hang of them," John said, picking up his fork.

"Watch me." Ed demonstrated. "You hold the bottom stick steady and use the top stick to pick." He picked up a piece of cashew chicken with the sticks and held it up in front of John who ate it off Ed's sticks. "You're in San Francisco now. "You'd better get used to using chopsticks. The last thing you want is to be mistaken for a tourist."

Midway through the lunch Ed needed to pee and excused himself to go to the restroom. "Get me a package of Marlboro's," John said. "I saw a vending machine right next to the restroom door."

"That's a filthy habit. Why don't you quit?" Ed said.

"I'm too busy trying not to be an alcoholic." John replied.

"Wrong answer!" Ed said and made the sound of a buzzer. Ed went to the restroom, and, when he came out, he bought a package of cigarettes for John. When he turned around there was a man leaning over their table talking to John. Even from the back he could tell it was Morris. He held back until Morris left before returning to their table. He dropped the pack of Marlboros on the table.

"You'll never guess who that was," John said.

"I know who it was."

"He wanted to know what we were doing here. I told him we were on our honeymoon."

"Well, there goes the element of surprise."

"He's with some old ex-boyfriend. They're going to Yosemite tomorrow. He invited us to join them."

"I hope you didn't commit. We don't know what's in store at Louis Gevant."

"I told him to call us later." They finished their lunch and left. The boy waiter was standing by the big glass aquarium where enlarged speckled fish swam past. He bowed slightly when John waved.

The Louis Gevant restaurant was in a brick building. No name was displayed on the dark green door, only the address etched on a round brass plate with a small knocker. The door was opened by a uniformed attendant, and the host took them to a table in an arbor like alcove.

John still had Yosemite on his mind. "I'd like to go. "I've never been to Yosemite. I've never even seen a mountain, except from a distance or looking out of an airplane."

"I don't think it's a good idea. I can't tell you why. It's just a feeling I have." The waiter appeared, and they ordered expensive cocktails. Ed had a Red Herring consisting of Vodka, tomato and pickle juice. "Louis Gevant is famous the world over for their Red Herrings," Ed told John.

"I think it must be an acquired taste." He took a sip of Ed's drink and made a face. "You still haven't given me a reason why we shouldn't go to Yosemite. It's the perfect opportunity to keep an eye on Morris. Far better than anything we could have come up with ourselves."

2PM came and went. John looked at his watch. "I think we've been stood up." Ed looked around the room, looking to spot someone who might be planning to meet them. The restaurant was dark and almost empty. "Now there's no reason not to go to Yosemite," John said.

"How did Morris just happen to stumble into us at Sydney Choo's? Don't you think that's an odd coincidence…our being there at exactly the same time?"

"He looked really surprised when he saw me. He asked if we were following them," John replied.

"Who's following who? Hunters becoming prey. Those stories don't usually have happy endings."

"You worry too much. I think you've got Morris all wrong."

Ed was speechless. He stared into those baby blue eyes, and words wouldn't come. What was happening? Had the person he loved most in the world suddenly gone brain dead or was a betrayal so monstrous so inconceivable taking place that Ed, even in his wildest imagination, could not conjure it? Ed finished his drink, and they left the restaurant. Ed was silent during their walk back to their hotel. John was bubbly, enjoying the sights, the dramatic hills cluttered with houses, the lovely bay dotted with white sails, the islands Alcatraz and Angel, the mighty Golden Gate Bridge, the finger shaped Coit Tower poking up above North Beach, the stately Palace of Fine Arts. "It's more beautiful than I ever imagined. I want to live here. Let's find an apartment to rent. I saw some signs on Divisadero."

At the top of Hyde Street they waited for a cable car. "What's wrong?" John asked, finally noticing Ed's silence. "Are you mad at me? Did I do something?"

Ed looked at John, disbelieving. "Have you forgotten why we're here? Why we flew to El Paso? Because I believe that Morris is a major player in some rotten, deadly scheme. He practically told me so himself. We went to El Paso to get evidence; so someone in authority would believe us. We flew to San Francisco following a dead end lead and who turns up? Morris? I think we're in mortal danger, and you want to go to Yosemite with them."

It was the first time that John had experienced anger from Ed. It shocked him into acquiescence. "Look! Let's go with them. We may be able to find out something. Meantime we'll keep our guard up and watch each others back. I promise I won't let anything happen to you."

"You're so trusting. Like a child. I have to protect you."

They hopped off the cable car, and John threw his arms around Ed. "We'll protect each other. There, it's settled." He found it hard to deny John anything. He felt helpless in the face of John's determination. Morris had somehow beguiled him, and there was nothing he could say that would make a difference. He looked at John, golden in the sunset rays, his dark hair a wild mop blowing in the stiff breeze coming off the nearby Pacific. His red lips begging to be kissed, his face radiant, his eyes beaming with love. Ed knew he had lost.

CHAPTER 33

Yosemite

The next morning there was a knock on their hotel room door while Ed was in the shower. He poked his head out of the bathroom door and asked John to hand him his clothes that he had laid out on the bed. He saw Morris with a boy younger than John. He finished drying off and dressed in the bathroom. When he came out they were gone.

"That was Morris," John said. "He got himself some chicken, not a day over twenty I bet. Name's Tommy Roy. He's as sweet as can be. A nice Southern boy."

"Why do Southern boys always have two first names? Joe Bob, Sam Willy, Billy Joe, I don't get it."

"Stop making fun of our fine Southern traditions. My mom used to call me John Will."

"I'm sure you were adorable," said Ed, rolling his eyes.

"I was a little devil. A real trouble maker. I didn't learn to be a heart breaker until much later."

"Where are they anyway?"

"Downstairs having breakfast. Are you hungry?"

"After that six course dinner we had at the Cafe Du Midi. I may never eat again."

Morris and Tommy Roy were still in the dining room when Ed and John came down with their backpacks. Tommy stood and took Ed's hand "I"m Tommy Roy. I'm sure glad to know y'all." Morris did not get up, but he looked up and flipped some keys to John.

"It's the silver Mercedes parked on the street about a half block up the hill."

John and Ed walked up the street together, found the car and put their bags in the trunk. "Did you see that look Morris gave me?" Ed said.

"Don't start." said John. "Let's just have a good time... please." They got in the back seat and waited for Morris and Tommy Roy. John looked at Ed who looked a little tense. He took Ed's hand and held it in his own. A few minutes later Tommy was tapping on the window with a huge grin on his face. A few minutes after that they were driving in traffic and within a few minutes after that they were crossing the Bay Bridge.

Tommy kept up a stream of chatter which was a relief to Ed who was reluctant to strike up a conversation with Morris. It was too awkward under the circumstances. Morris didn't have much to say either and focused on his driving. That left the coast clear for Tom Roy. You know I heard about this Yosemmy place way back in Alabamy. That's where my grammy lives with my Uncle Burt and a whole passel of cousins. I got more cousins than you can shake a stick at. Anyhoey, I heard this place was real purdy and all. We should go hikin'. I used to go hikin' down to the crick with my buddy, Amos. We fooled around a little, but I didn't know nothin' back then. Not like I knows now."

Morris reached over, took Tommy's head in his hand and turned it around to face front. "Help me drive. Look on the map. Where do I get the 45?"

Tommy opened the map but looked befuddled. "I dropped out of school before I took map readin'."

Morris pulled off the road, snatched the map from Tommy and studied it. He shoved the map back at Tom, pulled back on the road and floor boarded the accelerator until their car was shooting past all the other cars on the road.

Ed whispered in John's ear. "Why is Morris so irritated?"

"I misunderstood the invitation. It was only for me." John replied.

"Oh," said Ed. A tomb like quiet consumed the car.. Morris had turned off the radio when the stations started to fade, and no one was saying a word. Finally Ed spoke to Tommy Roy. "So you grew up in Alabama?"

"Reckon I did, but we lived in Mississippi the year Paw had a job in that sausage factory in Jackson."

Ed could see it all clearly now. Morris was mortified that he had been reduced to spending time with a cluck. What he wanted was John who was snuggled in the back seat with Ed between duffels and backpacks. The more Tommy Roy talked the redder Morris' neck became. In the park Morris got them registered, and then drove to the cabins which were at the other end of Curry Village. Morris parked, and they went to their separate cabins.

Inside their cabin John and Ed threw their bags on the bed, and John slipped a flask out of his. He passed it to Ed who shook his head and passed it back. John held out the flask. "Just one, please. I want to drink to us." This was something Ed couldn't refuse. It was loaded with meaning for him.

"To us!" John said, holding up the flask. "May we find everything we're looking for in each other." They both drank.

Ed was thinking how sexy John looked in his cut offs. He knew what was filling out those jeans. He had been there often enough. But before he could make his move there was a knock on the door. John got up and opened it. It was Morris and Tommy Roy.

Tommy busied himself looking around. "You guys got a nicer cabin. You got a shower. We got one of them big tubs with claw feet. My grammy had one of them."

"It's still early," Morris said. "We're think of hiking up to the top of Vernal Falls. Why don't you join us?"

"Let's," said John. "After that drive I need to unravel." Ed was reluctant. He wasn't ready to confront Morris, but he might not have a choice if they were alone together. He could see that John was eager, and there was no way he would let John go off with Morris without him.

They crossed the valley floor in conversational pairs. For a while he was paired with Tommy. He pointed out Vernal Falls, and Tommy's jaw dropped open.

"We're hikin' to the top of that mother? Bless my stars."

"It's not a hard trail" Ed said.

They climbed over boulders and scrambled over tree trunks that might have been tossed there in the last storm. At the trail head they began going up. There were a few others on the trail either going up or coming down. At one point Morris made them stop. "Let's let that bunch get further ahead. Then we can have some privacy." *What do we need privacy for?* Ed wondered. Below them the Merced River gurgled and leaped skipping over stones as it traversed the valley floor. Across the expanse of the Yosemite Valley Yosemite Falls plunged some 2400 feet. Great stacks of cumulus clouds glistened white against an azure blue sky. It was a lovely day to be out if only Ed could relax, lose this feeling of foreboding. As they continued up the Mist Trail, so named because at points they were enveloped by spray from the fall, Ed notice John looked pale and tense. "What's wrong?" he asked him.

"Nothing. I mean I suffer from vertigo. I'll be okay. We don't have to stop because of me."

"Let me know if you want a break." He put his arm around John and squeezed him a little. As he turned his head he got a glimpse of Morris watching them. They continued up the trail until they reached a plateau, a large expanse of smooth granite beyond which the Merced River churned toward the lip of the three hundred foot cliff and poured over in a mighty rush thundering as it went. They needed to shout to be heard. Morris climbed over a guard rail and waved for the others to follow.

John hung back, saying he couldn't go near the edge. He sat down between two saplings. Tommy Roy went off to see Nevada Falls which was a little ahead. Morris waited by the lip and beckoned to Ed. Ed walked over to where Morris was waiting, trying to stay on the driest part of the smooth granite, smoothed by eons of river rushing over it and very slippery for humans in their shoes.

He walked up close to Morris; so he could hear what he was shouting. "Jump!" said Morris.

"What?" He looked down to see the gun pointed at his belly.

"You've been a thorn in my side for too long. This has to end now. Do us a favor and jump; so I don't have to fire this gun and maybe start an avalanche. Do you want to be responsible for the deaths of innocent people?"

"Are you mad?"

"I didn't want to do it this way, but I don't think I have a choice. If I have to shoot you I will have to shoot John as well. Or anybody else that might be in sight."

"You are mad."

"So do us a favor and jump. I'm sure John will be grateful that you spared his life."

Ed looked down into the vortex, the usual scene of trees and rocks gave way to the maelstrom of fear and disconnected thoughts. As he contemplated the fate that would save John he had a glimpse of someone running, and as that figure drew closer he saw that it was John. A second or two later John swept past Ed, and pushed Morris whose footing gave way. As he began to fall he reached for something to grab and it was John. Together they sank into the foaming spray.

    Ed stood there in shock at what just transpired. He reached out as if to grab the sight and bring it back to never happened. John was gone, now a broken body lying among the jagged rocks. He couldn't bring himself to look. Tommy Roy appeared and walked up to Ed. "Where is everybody?" he asked.

CHAPTER 34

Ed and Cory Redux

Ed's heart lifted the moment the taxi turned onto the familiar street and moments later turned into the driveway of the familiar house. The driver got out and opened the trunk and pulled out two large bags. Ed carried in his arms a fabric covered box. Cory came out of the house, and they embraced. Then Ed put the box into Cory's hands and paid the driver. Cory stood for a moment, looking at the box and knowing. Then he grabbed Ed's arm and led him toward the house. "Let's get out of this killer Texas sun. You know people have been known to burst in to flames standing out in our sun. Or because the humidity is so intense they simply melt. You go out of the room, and when you return there's just a puddle of water where they were standing. It's the God's truth. If you like I'll swear it on the Alice B. Toklas Cookbook."

They settled in the kitchen. "I made a pitcher of margaritas on the off chance that you could be persuaded to get blotto with me." He poured from the handed Ed a tumbler.

Ed shrugged. "I don't....."

"It's a wake. *Borracho* is where it's at. Hell, you've been in Mexico way more than I have. I thought you'd want to get all sloppy sentimental with me."

"Okay. One drink." He held up his glass and said, "To our John…to our friend…to our lover…"

Cory put his hand on Ed's arm. "Maybe he was just too beautiful to live. Nature has a way of destroying perfection. A butterfly lives for only a day."

"I should have…" Ed started to say.

But Cory stopped him. "No recriminations. This day is not about us. It's a tribute to our John." Cory continued, "Ah, John, you and I had a great run. Ed was cheated. He never got to live with you. To get the bad with the good. I loved it all. Your morning breath. I even loved holding your head when you vomited, wiping your ass when you were too sick to do it yourself…

Ed found himself unable to listen further and went outside. Presently Cory joined him. "Does it even cool off at night?" Ed asked him.

"Not in August. We call it the melting month. Tourists melt all the time in August." Cory answered.

"Tourists come here?"

"Germans. They go anywhere."

"I can't do eulogy, Cory. I'm still hurting too much."

"It's okay, Babe. We'll take the ashes to Galveston tomorrow and dump them in the Gulf. He loved Galveston. It's what he would have wanted." Ed nodded. "Then come inside. I don't want to be alone with his ashes."

Inside, back at the table around which the three had so often gathered in the past months Ed downed his unfinished margarita in a single gulp. "So what's next?" Cory asked.

"I don't know. Maybe Mexico or Brazil. I've never seen Brazil."

"Why don't you stay here until you decide? I'd like that."

Ed looked at Cory. "Would you?" Cory nodded, putting his hand on top of Ed's. "Well, maybe, just for a few weeks."

EPILOGUE

Ed had no intention of returning to San Diego. The life he led there seemed to belong to someone else. His life for the past twelve years had been with Cory in Houston, but when Emmet died suddenly from a massive heart attack, he knew he had to attend his memorial. Some of the old crowd were among the people gathered in Emmet's little beach house. Gary Grimes, former debonair leading man, read from a book of poems Emmet had written. His sagging jowls and quivering turkey neck were perfect additions for his dramatic reading. He concluded by saying "Theater has lost a giant...a colossal giant gone..." He then became too choked up to continue, and Doretta was forced to snatch the book from Gary's trembling hands.

Doretta Spain had been Emmet's idea of a leading lady, and he tailored more than one of his plays to utilize her specific talents. She had perfected the withering glance, which was powerful enough to replace three pages of dialogue. More verbose playwrights would find this annoying, but Emmet was convinced that less was more and was certain it was the secret of his success. It had long been rumored that Emmet and Doretta had been lovers years before. Emmet's lifestyle seemed to refute that, but while never acknowledging this to be true, Doretta never let the rumor die. In all her stories of exotic places where she had performed there was Emmet. Coincidence? Maybe, maybe not.

Bill and Edna Bronson, those reliable character actors then, now aged and faltering with shaking hands and voices, unveiled a portrait of Emmet's theater years. While sounding his praises they described every play he wrote as a disaster. No one knew what they really remembered; the past being a blur for them all.

As one after another of the old crowd paraded to the orange crate masquerading as podium and spilled their memories of Emmet, Ed cringed at the cheapness of the affair. Emmet would be mortified. Ed began looking for an avenue of escape. He had more than enough. He knew he would not be invited to speak. Many still blamed him for Emmet's downfall, and he blamed himself for passively watching it happen. He decided not to wait for the ritual scattering of ashes. Once was enough of that. He was standing close to the door of the one room house, and he slipped out without notice. He felt he had paid his respects, and he didn't really care what anyone else thought about it.

On the drive back to his hotel Ed decided to stop at a Quick Mart, to pick up a couple of things he had neglected to pack in his haste to leave, having only learned of the memorial the day before. No one was in the store, except the desk clerk, a slightly plumpish man in his early thirties, already beginning to bald. Not the sort that would rate a second glance from Ed.

When he took the shave cream to the register the man smiled and said, "Hello, Ed. Remember me?" The man didn't look in the least familiar, but the voice was from an earlier chapter in his life.

"Frankie?"

"Yep. That's me. Fucking Frankie. I bet you're glad to see me again."

Ed had no intention of letting him know the results of his prank. Never would he give him that satisfaction. For a moment Ed was speechless, finally blurting out a mumbled "How you been?"

"Not bad. I was out of work for a long time, but now I've got this job. So I'm doing better."

Ed stood lost in time, the ticking of a clock on the wall seemed to drown out everything else. "You look...You've changed. I hardly recognized you." He heard himself saying.

"Too much hard living I guess." Other people call it a drinking problem. I've made the grand tour of all the rehabs and halfway houses and drunk tanks in San Diego. I wish they would lock me up." What could Ed say? He was staring at this train wreck of a person, the pasty, sallow skin with red blotches, the lumpy body, the thinning unkempt hair, the dishpan hands with bitten nails, the several missing teeth among the yellow ones. "Hey! I've been sober for eight months. I think I'm going to make it this time." Ed was pointing himself to the exit. "We should get together. Talk over old times." Ed took his change and headed toward the door. "Where are you staying?" But Ed was gone and didn't hear him.

www.ingramcontent.com/pod-product-compliance
Lightning Source LLC
LaVergne TN
LVHW091538060526
838200LV00036B/652